PLANET
of
HOPE

PLANET
of
HOPE

JERRY BELVO

Planet of Hope

Copyright © 2019 by Jerry Belvo. All rights reserved.

No part of this publication may be reproduced, stored in a retrieval system or transmitted in any way by any means, electronic, mechanical, photocopy, recording or otherwise without the prior permission of the author except as provided by USA copyright law.

The opinions expressed by the author are not necessarily those of URLink Print and Media.

1603 Capitol Ave., Suite 310 Cheyenne, Wyoming USA 82001
1-888-980-6523 | admin@urlinkpublishing.com

URLink Print and Media is committed to excellence in the publishing industry.

Book design copyright © 2019 by URLink Print and Media. All rights reserved.

Published in the United States of America
ISBN 978-1-64367-630-2 (Paperback)
ISBN 978-1-64367-629-6 (Digital)

29.05.19

ACKNOWLEDGEMENTS

I am grateful to the people who encouraged, inspired, and guided me in the process of writing and producing the books: *Planet of Darkness, Planet of Hope, and Planet of Peace*. I would particularly like to thank Catherine Carroll for her psychic ability, to Brandon Moore for his editorial assistance, and to Dave Bramel for his proofing skill.

Thanks also go to Jethro, a spirit, whose quotes are found at the beginning of each chapter.

I want to thank all my friends and family for their friendship and love.

They have touched my soul and are a part of who I am.

I know this is only the beginning of the journey and I invite my readers to explore it with me. Thank you for reading my books.

INTRODUCTION

Times were rough for the planet. With constant wars and other catastrophes, it had become a Planet of Darkness. Living in a coal mining town in West Virginia offered a young family a paycheck but little solace. After Jim's Dad and Grandpa died, his Mom did not want him to end up a victim of the mines. She wanted a better life and they moved out west to Colorado.

Jim grew up in Denver, married Doris who had a child named Edward, and together they had a son named Eric. She was an avid smoker, eventually got cancer, and died.

Severely depressed, he sought answers in the spirit world. The evolution of spirit became an obsession in his life. It moved him into areas of knowledge he never knew existed. He was searching for a way to restore hope in his life and to planet Earth.

Now a middle aged man, he is about to meet a young journalist who will want to write his biography.

THIS IS HIS STORY.

CHAPTER 1

"There is always another way of looking at things."

"Is this seat taken?" I asked a young woman whose papers were strewn over the table and her books on the chair. It was the only seat left in the coffee shop. This Saturday I was browsing through the metaphysical section in the adjoining book store. Not finding anything new I thought I would treat myself to a latte before going home.

"I'm sorry, no it's not," she said in an alto voice, reaching over to pick up her books.

"Thank you," I replied. She appeared to be a college student about my son's age, doing her homework. I sat my latte on the only bare spot on the table noticing she wasn't really studying. She was gazing around the shop, maybe waiting for someone. The heat of summer was gone, and the sun shining through autumn leaves seemed to place everyone under its spell.

"Are you expecting a friend?" I asked. "I'll move if you want me to." "No," she said with a smile. "I'm people watching. I will be writing a book soon, and I'm matching characters with their looks, before I decide who to put in my book. I graduated from college last spring and have a degree in journalism."

"Would you like to match my character with my looks to see how close you can come?"

"Sure," she replied, turning towards me. "That'll be fun. I work at the newspaper through the week and Saturday is my only day to people watch. Let me see. You are in your mid-forties. You have reddish-brown hair slightly grey, light skinned with some freckles, high cheek bones, and you weigh 175 pounds. You are probably Irish and are a doctor."

I said. "You are right about most, but you missed my profession and my age. I'm an accountant in my fifties."

She continued. "You have dark sensitive eyes with a hint of sadness. You must've been through some trauma recently, but you don't look that old."

She's good, I thought, to pick up on that.

"And you are married," she said triumphantly, a smile lighting up her face as though she had just discovered a secret.

"Good guess." I said. "I was married. My wife died of cancer five years ago."

"But you are still wearing your wedding ring."

"Yes, I just feel comfortable with it on. It's like she's still around. I should probably put it in the drawer, but right now it's part of me."

"That explains your sadness," she sighed.

"You are half right. I'm over the pain of losing my wife of twenty years, but my sadness is for my son who recently had a terrible auto accident in the mountains. It left me extremely depressed, the thought of possibly losing another member of my family."

"I'm so sorry," she said, her demeanor changing to one of tenderness. "It must be extremely difficult to lose family members."

"There's always another way of looking at things that happen in one's life. God doesn't close one door without opening another one." I said, remembering the dark cloud that takes over my reality when a loved one is sick or dying. It literally destroys me, and I didn't want to go there today. Changing the subject, I said. "Look on the bright side. Today I met you. It has made my day. Thank you so much."

She cleared her voice as if to say something important, then hesitated a moment before asking. "Would you mind if I studied your character further? My father died when I was in grade school. He was a policeman and was killed responding to a robbery. I never got to know him and I really don't know how an older man thinks and acts. It would help my book. What do you say?"

"Well, if we're going to be compatriots I think we should at least introduce ourselves," I said laughing. "I'm Jim Roberts."

"I'm Marilyn Mars," she responded, "future author, I hope." "You can be anything you set your mind to," I said.

"That's reassuring. I come here to sketch characters in my mind, imagine their inner secrets, and watch their facial movements. I think I'm getting good at it, but I'm having a hard time deciding on the story line, the vehicle I need to put it all together in a book. If I'm to get one published it has to have intrigue, emotion, excitement, and a good story line. It has to be something to interest a lot of people. It has to draw people in to the story. Publishers won't waste money on a book they don't think will sell lots of copies. It needs a good plot. If you tell me a little about what a mid-fifties widower in Denver does with his life it might give me some ideas to write about."

"Why not, I have nothing else to do today." I enjoyed the conversation, and spending a Saturday morning with a lovely young lady whose smile could melt any man's heart. Besides, someone wants to know about me. Most people I meet only want to talk about themselves. This was my lucky day.

"Where do you want me to begin," I asked? "Wherever you want," she replied.

I could tell she was new at this. Maybe I was her first interview. "Let me buy you a cup of coffee first."

"Okay, I'll have the house blend with cream," she replied.

I went to the counter, ordered two house blends with cream, and settled down to tell my story.

* * *

My grandparents came from Ireland, and they settled in the Appalachian Mountains in West Virginia. Grandpa worked in the mines. He introduced Dad to my Mom and they started dating. They married in 1938 and I was born in 1940 just before Dad was drafted. The Christmas after my first birthday Dad carved a wooden locomotive for me. It had big round wheels and a smoke stack. I played with it for a long time. It was my pride and joy.

When the neighbor boy said that people were dying in the war, it upset me. Why would anyone want to kill someone else? I didn't want to lose my Dad. I couldn't understand why anyone would want to die. Mom explained how people went back to God when they accomplished what they came here to do. She said we would all go back to God some day.

One day we received a telegram. Dad had been killed in the battle at Normandy. Mom cried and held me for a long time. I didn't understand what was happening, but I felt so sad. All I knew was that it hurt Mom. I had looked forward to the day when Dad would come home and we could play. Now I had nothing to look forward to, and my fear of dying made me want to hate God for taking my Dad.

We went to live at Grandma and Grandpa's house. One night I dreamed Dad was playing with me. I told Mom, but she said it was my imagination. He came often, but I didn't tell her, not wanting to hurt her feelings. I could even talk to him.

The following year Grandpa took sick. He stayed around the house coughing a lot. Soon he was bed ridden and shortly thereafter he died. Mom said it was black lung disease. I had lost another male figure in my life. The only relatives I had left were Mom, Grandma, and Uncle Bob.

Although I was too young to remember much about my Dad and Grandpa I saw pictures of them and imagined they were still alive. Mom said it was best to put them out of my mind but that was hard to do. 'God had other plans for them,' she said. Once I caught Momma looking at a picture of Daddy in his uniform. She kept it in a drawer. When she was not around I took it out and held it.

Uncle Bob was in the war also, but he didn't get killed. When he came home he bought a truck and hauled things for people. Jobs were hard to find, with so many soldiers returning home. One day Mom and Uncle Bob decided we would move to Denver. They thought jobs would be more plentiful in a larger city. Grandma wouldn't come with us preferring to stay in West Virginia with her friends, but Mom didn't want me growing up to work in the mines. I was already coughing from the coal dust cloud that often hung over the town.

We put everything we owned in the truck and departed on a Monday in March. The first night we pitched a tent in the woods. I couldn't find my locomotive. We searched the truck but didn't find it. I was upset and Mom told me she would have Grandma send it to me later. Over time I forgot about it.

Going through Ohio our truck broke down and Uncle Bob had to go to the nearest town for help. It was just a fan belt but we lost a half a day.

The second night in St Louis we rented a room where we could bathe and slept in beds. After we left there it took two more days until we saw the Rocky Mountains. We were real excited, stopped the truck, got out, danced, and hollered with joy.

When we got to Denver, Uncle Bob quickly got a job hauling produce from the depot to the grocery stores. I started first grade that fall. Mom went to work as a secretary for an accounting firm.

Uncle Bob got married when I was twelve and moved out of our apartment. I finally had a bedroom all my own. I got a paper route so that I could have spending money. It was great, having money in my pocket, but times were still rough as we had to get along only on Mom's salary. I gave her my money so we could pay the rent. Uncle Bob gave me a bike for Christmas that year to help me on my paper route.

One day at school a bully knocked me off my bike and proceeded to beat me up. I stood my ground best I could, but went home with a black eye and bloody nose. My knee was also bleeding from scraping it in the sidewalk. Mom was furious. Uncle Bob said I needed to learn how to defend myself, and decided to teach me how to fight military style in case it ever happened again. It gave me confidence. But mom said there was no reward in fighting, and the best defense was to make friends with my enemies. The bully and I did get to know each other, but I still had more fights.

Almost every Sunday Mom and I went to church. She wanted to make sure I had religion in my life. She called it our day together.

In the tenth grade we bought a house and moved to a new neighborhood. I'd grown to over six feet tall, and with my long legs I was rather good at track. It was a good outlet for my energy. Mom didn't want me playing football. My Dad died fighting and football was too much like fighting. Maybe she was too protective of me.

I paid my way through college working nights at a restaurant. I got my degree and went to work for an accounting firm. In fact I'm still working there.

* * *

"Am I boring you?"

"Not at all," Marilyn replied enthusiastically. "I'm very interested. Please go on."

"Okay, but please let me know because I have a tendency to just keep talking until I'm interrupted."

"No, it's all interesting. I can imagine my father telling a similar story."

I noticed her squirming in her chair and suggested we take a break. I needed to use the bathroom. When I returned from the bathroom she was standing outside inhaling on a cigarette. I didn't realize she was so tall, well proportioned with long auburn hair curled forward on the end. Her red lipstick coated the end of the cigarette dangling from her right hand. She wore dark tight clothes, webbed hose, heavy makeup, and eye liner typical of a college student. "Beautiful day, isn't it?" I said.

"I don't look forward to winter, but fall is my favorite time of year," she said. "I have always wanted to be a writer and felt journalism was the way to get started. That way I could work while developing my writing skills. I could live anywhere in the world I want and still write books for a living."

"Do you have a boy friend," I asked?

"Not right now, I dated a guy in college. He was a year ahead of me and moved back to his home town in Pennsylvania after he graduated. We kept in touch for a while. He flew back here for Christmas, but shortly thereafter he met someone else. Its better this way, a relationship would be too confining for me right now. I don't want to be stuck in one place. I want to travel."

"Marilyn, what does one look for when they decide to write a book," I asked?

"You need a good human interest story with excitement and suspense. Have you done anything special that people would want to know about," she inquired?

"What I have experienced in my life doesn't appear interesting to me although at the time the events occurred they were exciting and emotional. I guess most people don't think their lives are exciting, not like what they read in books."

Marilyn was contemplating a question not knowing exactly how to word it. "Let's suppose I decided to write about your life. If I used your name everyone would know it's you. You would need to think about what you want to tell people. Once it's in print with your name on it, the world will know your innermost secrets. How would you feel about that?"

"I guess I don't really have anything to be embarrassed about, but just the thought of anyone knowing my inner thoughts scares me."

"We could use your story, but change your name and location. That way people would read it not realizing it's you. After it's written we might even spice it up a bit. Think about it. I'll be here again next Saturday, watching people. If you want to join me we can discuss it further." She shook my hand and with a big smile went back inside to collect her things and left.

What an interesting morning this was. I would have a whole week to think about it. Events have happened in the last few years that would be interesting for people to read about, but a biography written about me? Maybe it would be too personal, too intimidating. I didn't tell her anything about the psychic side of me. Maybe she wouldn't be interested. Most people don't want to know about that.

* * *

The week went quickly. Without taxes to compute, my days were short at the office. It allowed me to leave early and enjoy the fall weather before winter set in. Saturday morning came quickly and she was waiting for me when I arrived. With coffee in hand I sat down next to her on a small café chair. It was crowded again but she saved a chair for me.

"Good morning. Have you thought about what we discussed last week," she asked?

"Yes, I have. I talked to a few people this week and they thought it would be exciting. Right now I'm uncomfortable using my real name. If you write a story about me maybe I can make that decision later. After I tell you my story you can decide what to put in the book, or if it's even exciting enough to publish."

She nodded in agreement, clicked on a tape recorder that she had brought with her and said. "I want to know more about you first. When did you get married?"

* * *

"I met Doris when I was twenty-seven. She was five years older, but it did not bother me. I told my friends I liked older women. I met her at a party. We clicked immediately. I liked the way she moved. She was wide in the hips, just like mom, and when she walked she swayed from side to side. She caught me watching her and accented the motion. We both laughed and introduced ourselves. It was literally love at first sight. She had long dark brown hair that fell over her shoulders and a birth mark below her left shoulder blade about the size of a quarter. It wasn't noticeable unless she was wearing a strapless outfit. She was coy, yet very aware. She wasn't loud, almost never raised her voice, but always managed to get her point across. The only problem we had, she smoked and I didn't.

Doris grew up in Fort Morgan. Her father ran off when she was ten, leaving them to fend for themselves. Her mother got a job waiting tables and had several boyfriends. She often left her and her younger sister at home alone. Doris picked up the cigarette habit early. It was easy. Her mom left open packs of cigarettes lying around. When she graduated she headed to the big city to make a life for herself. Her first marriage lasted two years. She said it was lust at first sight, but there was no substance as they were young and too much alike. There were no children so the marriage was easily dissolved. She married a second time and had a son named Edward. Her husband started running around on her, staying out all hours of the night, spending all their cash, leaving her to scrounge for money to pay the bills. She finally decided for the sake of her son to divorce him.

She went to work at Saint Luke's Hospital becoming the admitting clerk. Patients came to her to be checked in to the hospital. She had an empathetic and caring nature, and made them feel comfortable. She had worked there three years when we met.

Doris had an answer for everything and everything had its place. She was just missing a partner to make her life complete. I was drawn to her by those beautiful brown eyes that seemed to say we were soul mates. She fit perfectly in my arms.

Her son, Edward, was four when we married. He had a hardy laugh that made others laugh. I liked kids and we hit it off at the beginning, but I think he became jealous of his Mom's attention to me. We didn't bond as I had hoped.

Eric was born two years later. Edward was excited to have a baby brother, but Eric turned out to be like me, gentle in spirit, introspective, and not competitive. He liked adventures and stargazing. He was thinner, with reddish brown hair, and had a hint of freckles just enough to notice. Edward tried to get him to play football when he was four, but being six years older it didn't work. He was too strong and overpowered him. Eric lost interest and preferred to play alone. Edward soon found an outlet in school with boys his own age.

Doris loved competitive sports but I was more drawn to the personal challenges like skiing. When the Olympic Games were on I watched one type of sports, she watched the others. Edward sided with her on the competitive ones but I didn't mind. We were a family and I liked the way that felt.

Meanwhile, Mom had purchased a condo in a high-rise retirement community and was happy being with people her own age. When we visited her on Sundays we would go to church and have lunch with her, but we'd have to be home in time for football.

On Sundays during football season Doris and Edward would be glued in front of the television watching the Broncos play. During the game she smoked and drank beer. They hooped and hollered with every play.

One day Mom got a call from West Virginia. Grandma had died. She went to West Virginia for the funeral by herself. I wanted to go with her, but could not commit myself to the ordeal. I didn't want to confront the dark cloud that hung over funerals. It made me feel hopeless.

I was saddened by Grandmas death, but Mom said. 'There is always another way of looking at things. Maybe she's happier now in heaven with Grandpa. Whenever anything bad happened Mom always found a way to make it alright. Now whenever something happens that I don't understand I say that phrase. It helps me ignore the dark cloud that surfaces whenever I think about someone dying.

After Edward graduated he got a job working for a construction company making good money. He didn't want to go to college. He never liked studying and construction was good for him. It kept him outdoors and physically fit.

Eric was more studious and when he got older we bought him a telescope for Christmas. He liked watching the stars move through the heavens at night. One summer Eric and I camped out in the mountains where the sky was clear and stars shone brightly. In the city we couldn't get clear pictures of the stars. For his high school graduation we bought him a camera that fit on his telescope so he could take pictures of the stars.

Eric moved on campus when he left for college. Doris and I were alone in the house. The house seemed big without the boys, but in no time we managed to fill it with our things.

Doris and I had celebrated our 21st anniversary in September, and were planning a big Thanksgiving Dinner that year. We had lots to be thankful for, Eric in college and Edward getting engaged.

The day finally arrived. Eric picked up his Grandmother as she no longer drove. She had made her famous mashed potatoes with lots of butter and a homemade pumpkin pie. Edward brought his fiancé and presents for everyone. Doris cooked the biggest turkey she could find. It was a grand day. The two love birds were talking about marriage, buying a house, and starting a family. Doris and Mom started discussing names for their first born not caring whether it was a boy or girl. We all joined in coming up with weird names just to make everyone laugh. Eric told us about spending his first night star-gazing in the observatory. He was majoring in astronomy. They all left about eight. Doris and I cleaned up the kitchen. We were very tired but we had a wonderful time.

Everyone was coming back for Sunday's Bronco game with the Raiders except Mom. She wasn't interested in the noise or the smoke. Doris and Edward took their favorite seats in front of the television. The rest of us found ourselves around the kitchen table occasionally eying the television when something exciting happened. Doris and Edward were going strong as usual. The Broncos were behind the first half, but after half time they scored a touchdown tying the game. We all went into the family room to enjoy the commotion. Everyone was cheering when all of a sudden Doris started coughing. It was severe. I'd never seen it so bad. She had coughed a lot lately, but never like this. She rushed to the kitchen sink to spit and coughed up blood. Then she turned pale and weak.

I hollered for Eric to call 911 while I helped her into the bedroom. In a few minutes she calmed down feeling better, recovering some color in her cheeks. When the ambulance arrived she was having second thoughts about going, but I insisted. "This was serious," I said. The neighbors came out when they heard the sirens to find out what was happening.

Doris said. "If I'm going to be in the hospital I want to go to Saint Luke's where I work so I can be with my friends." They loaded her gently in the back, closed the doors, and left with sirens blazing. We were all concerned. I asked that we all pray for her and put angels around her to protect her. The game was over and we didn't even know the score. Everyone departed shortly thereafter.

I had caught Doris a few weeks earlier coughing in the bedroom and suggested she see a doctor about her cough. When I asked her again she made some comment about seeing a doctor at the hospital. I didn't really believe her, but whenever she made up her mind about something, there was nothing I could do to change it. I thought that someday I would lose her to cigarettes, but God please, not today.

CHAPTER 2

"No matter how dark the heart a light still shines."

"What happened to your wife?" Marilyn asked, bringing me out of my reverie?

"I must've wandered off. I'm sorry. Where was I?" "They were taking your wife to the hospital," she said.

* * *

I called Mom to let her know what had happened, and I left shortly thereafter for the hospital. When I arrived she was still in the emergency room. Later she was given a room in ICU and I was allowed to see her.

"How are you feeling?" I asked, upon entering the room.

"I'm okay, Honey," she whispered in a soft voice. She always called me Honey when we were alone. "I couldn't get my breath. It was a terrible feeling and it scared me. I'm not afraid of dying, I just fear the process," she said.

"Don't talk that way. I'm not ready to lose you," I said, putting my arms around her and giving her a kiss.

"Did the Bronco's win?"

"I don't know. Without you a football game has no meaning. Have you talked to a doctor?"

"I won't know the results of any tests until tomorrow when my doctor sees me. I'm afraid of what he might find."

"I know. You've been coughing a lot lately and I'm concerned. Is it time to give up smoking?" She avoided an answer. I sat with her until visiting hours were over and the nurse asked me to leave. I didn't want to go home alone. All night long I was awake worrying about her, praying for angels to protect her and for God not to take her. I remembered her saying. "If God wants me I'm ready to go." When it came to religion Doris knew exactly what she believed and there was no room for discussion.

The next day the doctors found not only emphysema but several tumors growing in her lungs. Tests showed some were malignant, and they gave her six months to live. My worst fears were coming true.

She refused chemotherapy and radiation treatments saying she would prefer to live one day at a time without having to worry about her hair falling out and feeling terrible from the treatments. They were unlikely to help much anyway.

That first day she had more tests and I stayed at her side. I wanted to be there for her and make her comfortable. This was a time in my life I felt totally helpless, and I could feel dark clouds forming over my world.

I thought to myself. It shouldn't be this way. There has to be something I could do to heal her, but I couldn't even get her to stop smoking. To the end she still craved cigarettes. Maybe I wasn't to interfere with God's plan, but I doubted He had any plan unless it was to make humans suffer? That just wasn't acceptable.

I took her home a few days later and fixed the bedroom so that she would have the whole room to herself. I slept in the spare room. Since it wasn't tax season I was given time off to take care of her. Eric was there to help also. Edward, his fiancé, and Mom were frequent visitors. He would bring his Grandmother to the house, and she would cook dinner for us. Bless her heart. Occasionally she stayed over.

Doris had many doctor appointments. Most were covered by insurance, but much of it had to be paid in cash. It was strenuous on all of us. If I could have cured her I would have given my life to do it. She continued to deteriorate. It was December and she wanted to celebrate one more holiday season with us. She was in good spirits on Christmas Day acting as though there were no problems. In fact she made it through the entire winter and into spring.

As her disease progressed I started feeding her, cleaning up after her, and bathing her. Each moment with her was precious to me knowing any day could be the last time I might hold and caress her. How important those moments are when you are with the one you love. It seemed I could never do enough for her trying to cram the next fifty years of love into a few weeks.

Edward and Ellen were married in May, and we attended the wedding together. Ellen and her parents handled the whole affair. All we had to do was show up, and that was a blessing. I wanted to make sure Doris had a wonderful day.

It was a beautiful wedding and a memorable occasion. Eric was best man. He looked good in his black tuxedo. Completing his first year in college he was ready to party, and party he did. Ellen's girlfriends were there and he found a place at their table, him and seven women. They were listening intently to his every word about the stars. What a charmer!

A few days after the wedding Doris began to fade. I think she was staying around just so she could see her number one son married to a fine woman.

She didn't want to die in a hospital even though her fellow workers were there for her. They were very kind and thoughtful, and constantly sent her flowers, fruit baskets, and cards. She passed away in her sleep. The next morning, May 15th, I went in to help her out of bed and she was gone. I looked at her lifeless body and cried.

At the funeral service her friends from the hospital showed up en masse. I appreciated having so many people honor her.

When the funeral was over I was relieved that she was finally at peace, but I could still feel her presence when I was home alone. At night it was so lonely. I tried to line up things to do. I went bowling one night with a buddy from work. Another night I went to a night club where people were dancing so I wouldn't be alone. I thought if I met someone I wouldn't feel so lonely.

Then when I got home I felt guilty for seeking friendship.

One night I went to bed early, at eight o'clock. I had taken some sleeping pills so that I would fall asleep. I thought that if I took the whole bottle I wouldn't have to worry anymore. As I contemplated the act I could feel a dark cloud descending on me. I heard Doris' voice and then saw her standing in front of me.

She said. "It's not your time Jim. You'll be with me soon enough. There are those who need you now. Your work isn't finished."

She was regularly in my dreams and in meditations. She always looked so beautiful. I would tell her what I was doing just like when she was alive.

On July 4th we had a little celebration. We set a place at the table just to honor Doris. The next day Mom called. She didn't want to talk in front of the others but she was very concerned for me.

She said. "When your father was killed in the war I too went through what you're going through. I know how you feel. Allow yourself to cry until you can't cry anymore. That's the way you heal. That's closure. Don't feel ashamed to go through it. Death is a part of living."

"Thanks Mom, it doesn't ease the pain, but I do feel better knowing you care. Maybe I'll go to church with you Sunday."

Then she said. "My condo association is having a pot luck dinner Saturday. If you would like to come, you can be my guest?"

"Thanks Mom, I'll think about it and let you know."

It wasn't a bad idea. At least I would have something to do. I called Eric to see if he wanted to go, but he had plans with his friends, so I went alone.

Mom brought her famous butterscotch pudding cups on a beautifully decorated tray for the pot luck. She knew almost all the residents and introduced me. I was amazed how many single women had condos in the building. Although many were mom's age there were several younger ones. I met some of them, but when the party was over I went home alone wishing Doris had been there with me.

* * *

Fresh coffee was being brewed, and I was pulled out of my reverie. "Do you want another cup of coffee Marilyn? It smells so good. I think I'll have another," I said standing up.

"That would be fine, but I want a cigarette to go with it. Do you want to go outside with me while I smoke?"

"It's a pleasant day. I don't mind." I went after the coffee as she headed to the door. I joined her with two cups in hand and continued my tale.

* * *

Doris and I participated as much as we could in school events. We went to Edward's football games and Eric's track meets, but for some reason Edward kept his distance.

Now that Doris is gone Edward and I have little contact with each other. I wanted a good father/son relationship, but it has been difficult. Maybe he resented me taking his father's place, or was jealous of my attention to Eric. His Mother's attention to me may have made him jealous. Just don't know. I had heard that sons sometimes resent their mothers giving attention to other male figures.

A few months after the funeral, I got a call from Ellen, Edward's wife. They wanted me and my Mother to come to dinner. Maybe my concerns were unfounded. On Sunday, mom and I arrived mid afternoon. Eric was there as well. After dinner and dessert Ellen announced she was pregnant. It was great news. I would be a Grandpa. How exciting. When a person dies another is born to take their place.

The birth announcement was good for me. In its own way it helped bring some closure for me.

On March 13th the following year Stacy was born. She had lots of dark hair and eyes that sparkled. I fell in love with her immediately. Ellen and her family had light brown hair, so the little one must take after our side of the family. Edward had dark brown hair, almost black. For a moment I thought the baby resembled Doris, but that was just wishful thinking. Anyway I'm now a Grandpa.

* * *

"Do they have any more children," Marilyn asked?

"Yes, they have another girl named Holly. This one has her Mother's looks and light brown curly hair. Edward would like a boy some day.

They bought a house not too far from her folks in the northwest end of town, and now I see less of them. I feel I have to make an appointment to see my granddaughters.

Marilyn, don't shut out your parents when you get married. They need to interact with their grandchildren."

"When I get married? That'll be the day. All I meet are creeps. I want someone intelligent to take home to meet my Mom."

"Good for you. Don't settle for less."

"Actually Jim, I have a date tonight. I hope he treats me better than the last few guys I dated."

CHAPTER 3

*"There is no such thing as salvation.
It is an illusion, a specific thought pattern to regulate societal behavior."*

Marilyn was having a cigarette in front of the coffee house when I arrived the following Saturday. I was happy to see her and said a cheery 'hello'.

I got my coffee and sat down at the table strewn with papers.

Momentarily she was back inside gathering her things. "How'd your week go, Marilyn," I asked?

"It went rather well. I covered some news events, but nothing made the front page of the paper," she replied. "Someday I'll get my big break."

"How was your date last Saturday? Did he meet your expectations?"
"We're going out again tonight," she replied with a smile on her face.

"How was your week?"

"Nothing exciting happened. The last few days I've felt depressed being alone in the house. It brought back memories of my religious up-bringing, and I thought you might like to know my view of life." I said.

"Yes, tell me about it." She said, as she reached in her purse to take out a tape recorder, and began recording the session.

* * *

"The death of my father and grandfather deeply saddened me during my early years. I couldn't believe that God would have deprived me of two important people in my life. I often thought about what it would've been like if they still lived, how my father and I would have played baseball and gone fishing together. He could've taught me how to become a man like him. Growing up without a father and grandfather put a dark cloud over my soul. I think this gave me my first doubt about religion.

Every Sunday Mom and I went to church, and we would occasionally read the bible together. I had read most of the Old Testament except when everyone was begetting everyone else. I didn't care about that. At Christmas we spent a lot of time reading the New Testament so I felt I'd learned a lot about the Bible.

The next event in applying my religious upbringing was when I was in the seventh grade. I had these physical urges. The only person I thought I could talk to about this was Uncle Bob but I was afraid he would tell Mom. I felt ashamed as I had read in the Bible about not giving in to temptations. I tried not relieving myself but it made me so nervous I wanted to climb the walls. Once I abstained for a week, but then I just couldn't continue. I felt that if God wanted me to abstain he would not have tempted me so seriously. I found no joy in thinking I would spend eternity in bliss just to make up for this suffering.

Am I being too blunt?" I asked Marilyn. If she'd been my daughter I never would've gotten on the subject, but I felt it was important to show why religion lost its meaning for me.

"No, I'm fine with it. It's important to the story so go ahead."

"Not being able to get an older man's view of how he handled it I felt guilty. I prayed every night asking that I be spared from this punishment that felt so good, then I had to relieve myself. What a hypocrite I was.

One night I got so worked up trying to abstain I couldn't contain myself. I was crying from fear I'd go to hell if I didn't stop. Then something happened that I'll never forget. My room lit up and I heard a voice. I could barely make out the figure, but I saw Him standing there in front of me. I'd swear it was Jesus. He said. 'Pay no attention to the Bible. It was written by well intentioned men, not by God. It's only a guide for you to live by. You answer only to God. He would never allow you to be tempted beyond your ability to handle it. If the church will not forgive you I will.' Then he was gone. After that I did what I had to do without being afraid I'd go to hell.

If the church was wrong about that what else were they wrong about? As you see, I was having doubts about my religion.

My next religious crisis happened in college. I was dating a girl named Joan. We'd been going together for some time and were having sex regularly. We had not thought about getting married, but I felt comfortable in the relationship, and had less anxiety. Again religion came into the picture because of having sex outside of marriage.

My roommates and I were having a discussion about religion and one asked me how long I was going with Joan, and if we were having sex? Without thinking about it, I said 'yes'. Then he gave me this, 'ah ha' look as if to say, I got you.

It made me quiver inside and I felt guilty. Why did he have to say that? It concerned me and I didn't know what to do. Finally it got the better of me and I decided to talk to Mom. After all I was an adult and should be able to talk to her in confidence, I thought.

When I told her she really got upset. "What if she gets pregnant? Have you thought of that? You would have to marry her. Do you love her?"

"No. Yes, I wasn't sure." Maybe it was not such a good idea telling her, but she did have valid concerns. "Mom we are careful. I don't think anything is going to happen."

"How do you know nothing's going to happen? It only takes once and it could ruin your college career, or at least make things more difficult for you."

She was right. I would have to think about it. I talked to Joan. She was surprised I mentioned it to anyone, and she wasn't too happy to be drawn into it. After that Joan and I drifted apart. If I wasn't going to marry her I certainly didn't want to get her pregnant.

It was back to the Bible, I just couldn't understand why two singles weren't allowed to have intercourse, but it was alright for married people to do it whenever they felt like it. The Bible had to be wrong. All I knew was I wanted to pick fights when my testosterone was high and was peaceful afterwards. It just wasn't fair to have this scourge in my life. I would have to put my excessive energy to work doing something more productive.

I started going to the gym. Working out helped relieve some excessive energy, but the gym was co-ed and the girls in their skimpy outfits didn't help the matter any.

Finally I graduated and got a job. My excessive energy was channeled on something productive, but at night I was out on the prowl. If I wasn't going with someone and having sex regularly, I was on the lookout for my next conquest.

Then I met Doris and my sexual energy was finally channeled into a relationship that would last. We got married and were happy together. She believed in God and had a Christian upbringing. She wasn't religious and we didn't go to church often, which was fine with me. I was slowly pulling away from the church anyway. However, I did want the boys to have a religious background. I thought religion was important in developing a person's moral fiber. So my Mom and I would take them. It gave her a chance to see them more often. I think it helped them create a genuine relationship with their Grandmother.

Every day I read the newspaper and watched the news. It seemed the only reports were on negative events. If this was a religious society why were so many bad things still happening to people? Had they not learned the teachings in the Bible? Could it be that the battles and wars mentioned in the Bible were self perpetuated? I couldn't accept God allowing wars to exist and taking kid's fathers when they needed them most. Couldn't people see that creating an enemy gave them a reason to hate? There had to be another way of looking at things.

* * *

I glanced at Marilyn. "Would you like a cigarette break?"

"Yes." She replied turning off the recorder and heading for the door.

I went with her. As we stood there enjoying the fall sunshine I said. "I hope I'm not boring you with this religious stuff, but I thought you would like to know about my background. Do you know anything about metaphysics?"

"Isn't that when something happens in spirit you can't explain, like when ghosts haunt houses," she asked?

"In a way it is, but that's only a small part of it. It does get all the publicity, but there's a lot more to it than that. I want to tell you how I learned about it and how it's affected my life," I replied.

A few minutes later we returned to our table with fresh cups of coffee.

* * *

About ten years ago I was becoming bored with life. It had to have more meaning. A person can't just go from one day to the next without some new mental stimulus. Since my religion had lost its spark I thought maybe I should check out other religions. Maybe it was just mine giving me a problem.

I went to the bookstore in search of a book that would tell me about eastern religions. I bought several books on Tibetan life, then Hindu and Muslim. It seemed everything was the same, only the names and locations changed. I felt churches were trying to push religion on the masses as a way of controlling them.

It wouldn't do any good for me to change religions. If I was going to have a religion I may as well stick with mine. At least I knew Jesus. He had appeared to me and I knew He was real.

On one of my trips to the bookstore I was checking out new age literature and bought a book which expanded my thinking into the spirit world. I began to understand such things as spiritualism, psychic energy, and vibration. They all had a purpose. I was fascinated by it and went back to the bookstore buying up every book on these subjects. After I had absorbed everything available I ventured into a metaphysical bookstore where I found more books on various topics of interest, healing, diet, massage, and various therapies.

I became a regular at the bookstore. The assistant manager was always there to help me. We had some good conversations on my frequent visits.

Doris knew I was reading new age books and was happy I found something that interested me, but to her it was just another religion. Everything to her had to be in black and white. If it wasn't she wanted nothing to do with it. One day I mentioned the black and white world to the store clerk.

"Do you have any information on the Black and White world versus the grey one?"

"I understand the black and white world to be the physical world, but what's this grey one?" She asked putting down the books she was carrying.

"To me the shades of grey are where you allow everyone to be as they are, like in the spirit world where everything just is. My Mom always said. 'There is always another way of looking at things,' and that says a lot to me. Allow people to be as they are. Don't try to fit everyone into the same mold. Let everything unfold as it's intended. When you push something it seems to always turn out wrong. Like fine wine it needs to age. Allow time to perform. The impurities filter out and the wine becomes clear."

"I like the word 'filter'. It's the key, the filter you are looking through is your perception," she said.

"That's good." I replied, then said, "I've been coming in regularly, and I have gotten to the point I find nothing new on the shelves having read everything. The new books have a different title but the message is the same. I want something totally new. If you would let me know when something really new comes in, I would appreciate it."

"Sure, I'll keep you in mind. Your idea of black and white is a different way of looking at things. You should write it down. Whenever a new concept comes along write it down. Your ideas are as good as anyone else's."

That was a vote of confidence. From that day forward anytime I had a new idea or revelation I wrote it down.

* * *

One day at the metaphysical book store the clerk mentioned a seminar that was going to be held and suggested I go to it. I talked it over with Doris and we agreed it might be good for me. The seminar was on Mind Control. A book had been written that was being used to conduct seminars on how to use your mind more fully. I was skeptical at first but as the seminar progressed I became a believer.

The first part of the seminar was on meditation. We created a peaceful place in our minds where we could go to find answers to problems and to rid ourselves of unwanted energy. I imagined an elevator in which I traveled up to a space platform. It had a desk, a workbench, chairs, mirrors, and green plants. It even had a hot tub.

Each day of the seminar we would meditate in our peaceful place. One day in front of a mirror we visualized anger, rage, anxiety, and stress oozing out of our body until it looked like a dirty coat. We unzipped this outer coat seeing ourselves as pure, clean, and free of impurities. Then we threw the oozing coat into the fire and watched it burn. We looked at ourselves seeing a perfect body, smooth skin, just the right height and weight. This was the real me the one I should always imagine, healthy, wealthy, and youthful.

Another time we sat at our desk and wrote down the most recent problem we were having. Then we wrote all the potential ways to resolve it. We invited the image of someone we were having a problem with into our safe place and resolved the issue by mutual agreement.

In another part of the program we were assigned a partner. They would say a couple of words. You would look into their eyes and tell them what they were thinking. I was good at reading their thoughts. Most of the group could read other's thoughts, but I didn't feel one had to be a psychic to do these things.

We also listened to our bodies to determine actual Truth. We would tell a lie and sense our body's reaction to it. Then we would tell the Truth and feel the reaction. It was amazing how accurate we were. Someone else would tell a lie and we would feel a reaction. After learning this technique no one has ever been able to lie to me without me sensing that something is wrong. I may not be able to put my finger on it, but I know they are lying. That's true even for politicians. If their words don't give them away their eyes do.

I was happy with the results of the seminar and signed up for an advanced course. This course enabled me to take control of my life and to be responsible for everything that happened to me. I could no longer be a victim.

Me, Jim Roberts, the victim, no longer existed. If I was stressed I knew how to handle it through meditation. I learned how to speak up for myself. If someone lied I knew not to trust what they were saying, and I learned how to look a person in the eye and know if they could be trusted.

I took Doris to my graduation in which we each gave a testimonial. She said I was a different person and she liked what she saw, but I couldn't convince her to take the course.

* * *

Looking at her watch, Marilyn interrupted me saying, "I have got to go. I have a date tonight and much to do before he arrives. I like him, but I can't get a handle on our relationship. One minute he is all over me, the next he is distant."

"Don't rush it. If it's meant to be it will be. You are a good catch," I said winking at her. "If I were younger I would give him a run for his money."

She blushed and said, "Thank you. I'll see you next week."

"See you next week," I said in response. Then we left. I thought to myself. 'She is such a fine person. I wish I had a daughter like her. She would make me proud. I hope he doesn't hurt her.'

CHAPTER 4

"One does not pass from this plane until they have experienced the pain they inflicted on others."

I saw Marilyn sitting there, eyes down as though deep in thought. "Good morning. Sorry I'm late," I said. "Do you want some coffee?"

"No, I'm fine," she replied.

I got a cup for myself and sat next to her facing the window looking at a graying day. The air was starting to chill. I hoped it wouldn't rain, even though we could use it. "Shall I begin," I asked?

"Sure," she said turning on her recorder. She seemed preoccupied, not her usual bubbly self, not people watching as she normally did.

"If you want to skip a week, we can do that," I suggested. "No, I'm ready, go ahead."

* * *

One day shortly after Doris died I decided to go to the book store to check their calendar of events to see if there were any seminars to attend. I wanted to continue expanding my horizons, and needed mental stimulation. The words *New Age* were over used. Every age was new, but it was the only term everyone seemed to understand. The assistant manager mentioned she had a psychic friend, Carolyn Turner, who was planning to hold weekly meditations. Maybe it would be to my liking.

"It sounds interesting," I said.

"I have her phone number somewhere," she said looking through the papers on her desk. "Carolyn changed numbers recently because she was being stalked, but I won't go into that. She'd have to tell you about it."

I thought. "Why would a psychic be stalked?"

"Oh, here it is," she said pulling it out from under a stack of papers. "She doesn't want it given out freely to anyone, but since you are a regular customer I'll give it to you. Tell her I gave it to you."

I thanked her and went home. That evening I called Carolyn, and she agreed to meet me at a coffee house in her neighborhood.

The next evening I was at the coffee house promptly at six in the evening. A tall slender woman with blond hair was sitting alone by the window sipping a cup of tea. She was wearing a pair of sun glasses.

"Are you Carolyn Turner," I asked approaching her table? "Yes, are you Jim Roberts?"

"Pleased to meet you," I replied. "It is exciting for me to meet someone like you."

"I hate to appear so aloof, but I'm being stalked," she said. "Who would stalk you," I asked?

"The police," she whispered for my ears only.

Lowering my voice, I said. "How unusual. Shouldn't they be protecting you? How did it happen?"

"I was working with them to find missing objects and people. Whenever they needed a psychic to aid them in their searches they'd ask me. Last time they called I thought it was going to be the usual search, but they had ulterior motives in mind. They were investigating one of their own and didn't tell me. I led them to a location where they found stolen items which linked him to the crime and they arrested him. He's now out on bail and I was getting threatening phone calls. I moved across town and changed my number. I'm not working for them anymore. It's too dangerous," she said shaking her head. "Life's short enough as it is. I wanted to move as far away as possible without leaving town altogether. It's been hard on my business though."

"I'm sorry to hear of your trouble. I hope you're never in that position again. What do you do for a living?" I asked.

"I give readings and perform healing rituals for people. It usually keeps me busy, but I had to contact all my clientele to let them know that I moved. Some of them wouldn't drive across town and I lost them."

"What about you," she asked? "What is your background?"

"I'm an accountant. My wife recently died of cancer leaving me with two grown sons. The oldest, Edward, is a contractor. He got married just before Doris passed. Eric is in his second year in college and lives near campus.

Carolyn said. "What makes you seek enlightenment?"

"I don't have a religious affiliation anymore. I believe in Jesus, but have a hard time accepting my wife's death as divine will. It's also difficult accepting the religious dogma of organized religions. I want to accept everything on faith and be done with it, but I'm too logical, and blind faith isn't logical. My mind processes information through two different filters, one black and white, the other shades of gray. Most people live in a black and white filtered world. It allows them to feel secure without having to use the gray filter until some catastrophe happens that can't be explained. Then they call it God's will."

She sat quietly taking it all in then asked. "What are you calling a grey filter?"

"I recently read that when a couple wants a child, a spirit is drawn from the ethers to them through a gray filter. The spirit makes itself known and the couple feels its presence which makes them want to conceive. When the child is born it begins bonding with the parents which makes it feel safe. As it develops it picks up information from the parents on what feels good and what doesn't feel good. In this way it slowly closes the filter to the gray world and moves into the black and white one."

"But, what happens if the parent can't provide for the child or if the parent is abusive or non-attentive," Carolyn asked?

"Then the child finds safety in the gray world. It holds on to its psychic abilities, sees spirits, and communicates with what we call the unknown."

"It makes good sense, Jim. If someone goes through a traumatic incident, such as a major illness, divorce, or death of a partner they open the gray filter and see life from a different angle. They become more accepting of others and maybe even communicate with the departed. I want people to at least be open to this philosophy. If people can learn to communicate with their guides it might bring peace and understanding to the masses."

Carolyn continued. "As a psychic I know a lot about the grey world of spirit and I know how you feel. I want to start having weekly meditations, maybe on Thursday nights. We could meet every Thursday at my place. If you're interested I'd like for you to attend."

"That sounds great. You can count me in. This could be what I'm looking for, and it would be good for me to get out and be among people for a change instead of staying home at night."

"I'll call you after I speak to a few other people," she said as she got up to leave.

"Yes, do call." I replied. She nodded, "Yes."

"It was a pleasure meeting you." "Likewise," she said as she departed.

* * *

It was two weeks before I heard from Carolyn. One morning she called my office to invite me to a meditation on Thursday evening. She gave me her new address and I agreed to be there.

Thursday night I planned to get to her place early before the others arrived, but two women, one named Ouizi, short for Mary Louise, and the other named Sara Lightfoot were already there. They were sitting on Carolyn's back patio in the shade. She poured me a glass of fresh made tea as I sat to join them. Sara mentioned meditating in the mountains the previous weekend communicating with her Native American ancestors. She had gone camping with her husband and their German shepherd. Others joined them at the campground. They sat around a small campfire, and smoked a peace pipe.

Carolyn brought out a tray of snacks for us to munch on. Ouizi, a petite woman with long auburn hair tied in a bun wore horn rimmed glasses looking very much like a librarian. She had allergies all her life, and brought a box of tissues with her which she constantly used. Sara was a little taller than Ouizi, had black hair and was heavier set. Her Indian features were pronounced with high cheek bones and a slightly rounded nose. They were both teachers in the public school system. At about 7 we went to the living room and sat in a circle.

Carolyn opened the discussion by asking each of us to tell about ourselves. She mentioned about her upbringing, having parents who abused her and having to hide from her father who would get drunk and hit her and her sister. Her mother died when she was young. The two girls spent a lot of time with their grandmother who tried to protect them from their father. Carolyn was a psychic from the very beginning having imaginary playmates, seeing spirits, auras, and often playing in that secret place in her mind.

I had never known a psychic before. I could only imagine how it must be to see spirits and feel different energy.

One by one we took our turns telling how we became involved in the search for meaning in our lives. We then discussed important happenings from the past week, important things that made a difference in our lives, such as promotions, loss of clients, illnesses, and psychic occurrences. Anything that resulted in anyone using their mental or psychic abilities to effect change was viewed with great interest. When we were finished, Carolyn led us through several rituals. They were designed to relax us and put us in touch with our higher selves.

Then she led us through a healing ritual. Ouizi wanted to be first to see if it would help her allergies. She lay on her back on the carpet as we placed our hands on energy points on her body. Carolyn showed us where these points were, indicating the head, feet, joints and central body. We mentally saw the person releasing blockages of dark energy where the pain was occurring, until we felt it flowing freely. She turned over, and we sent energy up and down her spine by moving our hands over her. Carolyn then used a pendulum over Ouizi's body to see if there was any more foreign energy present.

Negative energy is taken on from others when a confrontation occurs, or when one has been in a tense situation like arguing with the boss, involved in road rage, watching disasters on television, or going to a funeral.

We all took our turns lying on the floor. It was very relaxing and I didn't feel like getting up when my turn was over.

Then it was time to meditate. We sat in comfortable positions with our shoes off. The lights were turned off but light still came through the window making for a quiet, peaceful setting. She told us to meditate on seeing successful conclusions to events in our lives.

We then settled back and became quiet. My mind wanted to work overtime and I had a hard time silencing it. I suddenly realized that maybe those voices were not mine. Just maybe I was hearing spirits in my mind. But as time passed, the voices became subdued and finally silent. I thought I had fallen asleep when Carolyn stirred. Not wanting to make any noise for the others I waited with questions about the voices until everyone's attention was back in the room.

Carolyn looked around the room at each of us. As she stared at me she said. "You have a light blue aura. It's a sign of peace. You also have someone with you. I see them over your left shoulder. It's a woman, maybe your wife. She has long flowing hair and a radiant smile. She wants you to know that she's alright and at peace, also something about a favorite ash tray, about not needing it anymore. Anytime anyone thinks of a spirit they are drawn to them. You've been thinking of your wife," Carolyn remarked.

I wished she hadn't commented on the ash tray. It reminded me of all the times I tried to get Doris to quit. Now she was gone and not smoking. How I wished she were still alive and lighting up a cigarette.

When it was Sara's turn to talk she mentioned seeing auras of various colors around us and told us what each one meant. Then she individually gave us private information.

Carolyn asked. "Does anyone have anything they would like to discuss about their meditation?"

I said. "I heard voices in my mind and had a hard time quieting them down. I thought maybe they might be the voices of others."

Carolyn replied. "That's always possible, but most of the time they are vibration patterns playing themselves out, kind of like residue left over from a hard days work. When a person meditates regularly quieting their mind first, a voice would signify someone else wanting to communicate. We should all get to that point of total silence eventually."

"Next week we will discuss going to a peaceful place in our minds, a place we can rejuvenate ourselves," Carolyn said.

My mind was full and I needed to digest what I had learned. "Is there anything you want us to bring next week," I asked?

"Just snacks. There's another person who will be joining us next week.

He has some very interesting things to tell us about some secret writings."

That sounded mysterious and intriguing. I thought, 'I'm going to enjoy this group.' We said our good-byes and departed around ten.

* * *

"Marilyn, today as I look back on what I have learned in the last five years it doesn't seem like a big deal, but it was mind boggling then."

She'd been taking notes even though the tape recorder was on trying to keep track of my story. "Shall we meet here again next Saturday," she asked?

Again I asked. "You seem to be preoccupied today Marilyn. You didn't even take a cigarette break. Is something bothering you?"

"It's nothing," she said.

"You can get by telling that to others but not to me. Remember, I'm sensitive to energy. What is bothering you? Why the long face?"

She thought for a moment bowing her head. Her dark hair flowed forward covering her face. She swept it back and looked up at me. "I started dating a guy. I thought we were getting along well together. He's already dumped me."

I tenderly put my hand on her arm, "I'm sorry, how did it happen?"

"We were supposed to meet for dinner. I waited an hour for him but he didn't show up. When I called his cell phone I heard another girl talking in the background. He said he was alone and just forgot, but I know differently."

"Marilyn, when the right man comes along you will both know it. You don't have to settle for anything less. The chemistry wasn't good with this other guy. You would have dumped him sooner or later, but he just beat you to it. I wouldn't lose any sleep over it."

"Thanks. It just hurts being dumped."

"It happened to me. I guess it happens to everyone at some time or other," I said. "I think we get a chance to experience it on both sides."

"But I liked him. I thought things were going well. I'm so glad I can talk to you. I'm sure that's what my father would have told me."

"You feel like the daughter I never had. Do you want to hear a story to cheer you up?"

"Sure, but I'll have that cigarette now." She shut off the recorder and made for the front door as I made my usual trip to the men's room and joined her in front of the shop to tell my story.

* * *

"When we first arrived in Denver Mom got a job and left me at the apartment in the care of an elderly woman who watched over me during the day. One day I was sitting outside on the porch steps, elbows on my knees and face in my hands peering out at the street when I saw a small turtle trying to cross. Instinctively I ran to the street, picked it up, and brought it into the apartment. The woman wouldn't let me keep it, so I took it out back and put it in an enclosed area. That evening I showed him to Mom and asked if I could keep him. She saw how excited I was and said 'yes', but it would have to stay outdoors, and I would have to feed and take care of it.

I asked her to name him and she suggested Happy because it was happy it didn't get run over. So every day I took care of Happy and each day Mom would say. "What made your turtle happy today?" It became a game and I would think up ways it made me happy and give those reasons to the turtle. This went on for a couple weeks. My sadness disappeared and Mom noticed the change. She said, 'See, you made the turtle happy and now the turtle makes you happy.'

One day I went out to feed him and he was gone. He had burrowed under the fence and had disappeared. With tears in my eyes I told Mom about Happy, and she said, 'Happy made you happy being your pet, now you must make him happy by giving him back his freedom,' and that is the end of the story."

"Marilyn, be happy you are free. He didn't make you happy." With that she smiled. "My suggestion is that you go out tonight with a friend. Don't try to find a replacement, just have some fun. Is there anyone you could call?"

"Yes, my friend Emily. We've been best friends since high school. Maybe she isn't doing anything tonight. I'll give her a call."

"Great, see things are looking up for you already. I wish you the best of luck."

"Jim. Thank you for doing this."

"You are welcome," I said heading to my car.

CHAPTER 5

"We have a child deep within us in need of love and understanding."

During the week I found a pamphlet and pictures I had forgotten about. I wondered if Marilyn might like to see them. On Saturday I took them to the coffee shop. She was sitting there sipping coffee when I arrived. She got there early to beat the crowd that gathered so she could get her favorite table.

"Good morning," I said cheerily approaching her. "I brought something for you to see. How are you today?" She seemed to be in good spirits and a little more bubbly than usual.

"I feel really good. I have already had a cup of coffee and talked to people I hadn't seen before. You know, when a person wants to they can make lots of friends right here in this shop. I already bought your coffee." She said, picking it up and handing it to me.

I sat down and took a sip. "It's great seeing you so enthusiastic. Your eyes are sparkling this morning. How'd your Saturday night go last weekend?"

"It went great! I called Emily and she was happy to hear from me. She had no plans so we went out on the town. When two people go out together it's easier to meet guys than when you are alone. We're planning to go out again tonight."

"I know what you mean. When I go out I'm usually home in a half hour. I just can't sit around doing nothing. I feel too conspicuous not having someone to talk to." I changed the subject. "Would you like to do something different and take a walk in the park this morning? This October weather is my favorite. The aspens are turning in the mountains. Their golden color scattered among the evergreens under a deep blue sky makes this the most peaceful place on earth."

"I'd love to go, but let me see what you brought me first," she said reaching for the pictures I had placed on the table. Her smile turned into a questionable frown. "These pictures are blurred. What are they about?"

"It's the blurred areas you are supposed to notice. Carolyn gave them to me. Those areas are from reflections picked up by the flash. Notice they are circular and appear to be moving. She told me they are of a psychic nature possibly startled by the flash of the camera. It means they have some sort of intelligence, kind of like a spirit that was caught off guard. See, this second one originates at the person's head and trails off. Carolyn explained that spirits siphon energy off people when they least expect it. When she does readings for people she sees this all the time."

"How interesting. I've seen pictures of auras around people, but never saw an actual spirit in print before. What are these papers?"

"I'm learning that when I pose a question before going to sleep I wake with the answer. One night my question was about creation and reincarnation. I found the answer so profound I wrote it down so I wouldn't forget it. I thought you might enjoy reading it," I said handing it to her.

She read silently,

> *God sat in the heavens, watching man grow, wither, and die repeatedly like a flower that grows from a seed, which explodes into a thing of beauty, and withers after producing its replacement. Man asked his creator for help, but God sat on His throne unmoved by his pleas. Interaction was non-existent so man did what he wanted without guidance because his pleas went unanswered. His desire to survive made him greedy. He took what he wanted, even killed for it, and the world became a* **Planet of Darkness**. *Eventually God got tired of His creation and destroyed it.*

*One millennium He decided to let creation evolve on its own? He created a spirit in His image, gave it the ability to evolve and multiply. This way He could experience creation as it evolved. Events would be conceived in spirit first before they occurred physically. Spirit gave the flower a root to help it survive harsh winters and spring forth each year. It would have seeds so it could multiply on its own. Spirit then brought forth man and guided him wisely. Every day was different because it evolved from the day before. Yet, man continued to harbor a gene called greed and was unwilling to serve his parent. Man still wanted independence, and when he failed to listen, death was waiting. Spirit retained the memory of man's accomplishments. This created a **Planet of Hope** that one day God's creation would be complete because spirit could evolve with each new incarnation.*

*Humans with different goals would over time exhaust possibilities unless God added other genes to the mix. Maybe He could blend spirit and man together into one form. It would advance evolution. It would bring about a **Planet of Peace**. It would take the cooperation of all three, God, Man, and Spirit, working together to accomplish this feat, this chapter of evolution has not yet been written, but the seeds have been sown.*

"Very interesting," Marilyn said. "It's a good theory, but I need to let it sink in. When it's not scientifically proven it's hard to grasp."

"That's why they call it metaphysics, because it goes beyond physics, but I would like to think it's worth pursuing. Some day the earth will cease to exist. When that happens, science won't help and God will be starting all over again. I don't think He will allow that to happen. I think spirit will take the memory of all that has been accomplished on the Earth and recreate it on another planet," I replied.

"I need time to digest this idea. Shall we go to the park?"

"We can take my car if you want, but it's only a short distance. We could walk," I suggested. "OK, let's walk."

* * *

One Thursday night we gathered at Carolyn's home again for another meditation. She had said we would be having a new member join the group that evening and she was quite enthused about the new person. "He would have a lot to offer the group, a lot of potential incites," she said. When I arrived he was already there. His name was Charles Martin.

"Hi, I'm Jim Roberts, pleased to meet you," I said shaking his hand. "Carolyn tells us you have some interesting things to share with us about your Uncle John."

Charles was in his late forties, a tall, well proportioned, athlete, with short black hair slightly graying on the sides. "My Uncle was an unusual man with lots of incites. He disappeared several years ago leaving many esoteric documents behind.

"What do you mean disappeared," I asked?

"Just plain vanished. One day he was there, the next, gone. Uncle John was into remote viewing, spirit and time travel. He could move through the galaxy recording information where ever he went. A lot of it I don't understand, it goes over my head. I'm just now getting his house ready to sell and need help organizing his writings. I didn't want to disturb the house until I have all of them documented. When I'm in the house I feel he's looking over my shoulder. I'm hoping that by coming to these meditations I'll meet others who may be interested in his writings."

"You have come to the right spot, and Carolyn knows everyone in town who works with spirits."

"I was a little concerned coming here because I don't want to be involved in witch craft," Charles said nervously.

"You don't have to worry about that. None of us here are involved in the black arts," Carolyn volunteered. She overheard our conversation. "Why not have your wife help organize your Uncles papers," she asked?

"She's pregnant. We're expecting our third child in four months. We think it's going to be a boy," he said.

Just then we were joined by Sara and Ouizi. I introduced them to Charles as Carolyn poured us some tea, and we sat down in the living room.

Charles felt right at home and told us more about what he was doing and how he wished he had someone to assist him in organizing his uncle's writings. Almost without hesitation Ouizi volunteered. Charles offered to pay her for her time and arranged to meet her the following week.

We hadn't had rain for over a month and the forestry department was warning everyone about possible fires, so tonight Sara was going to lead us in a meditation to bring rain to the area.

Sitting in a circle in the living room Sara said. "One thing a seeker has to understand is that whatever happens they have to believe that they've had a part in it. There's no room for doubt. If one is going to help the planet they have to understand they are a part of the planet and therefore crucial in its outcome. For the meditation it's important to think rain, feel it, and then let go. If anyone doubts the ceremony it can hinder the results." No one spoke up. "Let us begin."

We sat quietly for a few minutes until we had a chance to communicate with our higher selves. Then she quietly begin, "Picture yourselves standing tall, arms outstretched growing taller and taller, so tall that you are able to hold the moon in your hands." She paused for a few minutes as we visualized ourselves expanding to enormous heights. "Now picture yourselves in the Pacific Ocean, feet on the bottom and holding the moon. See yourselves as greater than life itself. You are all powerful." I'd never had this experience before. The feeling was overwhelming. Pausing for a few moments she then said. "Visualize a huge sprinkling can. Dip it into the ocean until it is full. Move slowly towards shore. See the coast line then visualize Colorado. Pour the water slowly where you want the rain to fall. Now feel the rain on your face and in your hair as it is falling. Feel the wonderful cleansing power as it puddles and runs down the street. See everything growing brightly and then feel at peace. You are one with the earth." There was another pause. "Know it is complete."

There were pauses so that we had a chance to visualize each step to get the full effect of what was happening.

We stayed in meditation for about an hour, thinking about and seeing it rain peacefully around us. One by one we opened our eyes not moving or saying a word until all of us were finished. Instead of taking mental journeys like last week we spent our time thinking rain.

After we came out of meditation, Carolyn explained to us that such secrets as creating weather won't be understood by mankind as long as one is allowed to interfere with the destiny of another. When man evolves beyond his ego these secrets will be common knowledge, but only those beings that have the ability to blend with the wind and feel the heartbeat of the planet will be able to access this knowledge. Rain is not for man. It is for the cleansing of the planet.

"Before we break up tonight I want you all to visualize the third eye in your forehead. When you meditate it opens to new ideas and has a tendency to stay open. Before you leave close it down so no unwanted thought energy is attracted into it." Carolyn raised her right hand and made a few clockwise circles above her eyes. We mimicked her pattern.

At ten o'clock we said our good-byes. Carolyn said to Charles, "You are welcome to come back to meditate with us any time."

I walked Charles to his car and asked him. "Will we be seeing you again? I think your energy blends well with ours. Three women and one man makes for unbalanced energy."

He agreed and said. "I'll be here next week. Ouizi is going to help me get organized. I just haven't had time to do it myself and until I learn more I don't know where to begin."

"I'm sure she'll do fine. It was a pleasure to meet you." "Likewise, I'm sure," Charles replied.

On the way home I thought Charles' friendship was worth cultivating, and I was enthused by the prospect of someday reading his Uncle John's work.

* * *

Looking at Marilyn I said. "Carolyn opened the door to my metaphysical journey. It's like being in spirit school, and I was learning the tools of the trade, so to speak. When I met Charles and he introduced me to his Uncle's writings it put a whole new light on the subject.

Charles Martin is a technical engineer living near Broomfield, Colorado with his wife. Besides his parents, Uncle John is his only other relative. He spent time with him when he was a kid and found his stories fascinating. Uncle John had given him a key to his house and made him executor of his estate.

They spoke regularly on the phone, and he often looked in on him.

His wife Betty was taking care of Uncle John's yard when he disappeared but after several seasons she lost interest. She hasn't been to his house in a year as her children demand too much of her attention."

"This is good information, but I have to go," she said clicking off her recorder. Shall we meet again next week?"

"Most definitely we shall. Same time, same place," I replied. "See you then."

"Good-bye," she said as we walked out the door.

CHAPTER 6

*"We only pass this way once.
Are we going to be a beacon to light the way?
Or, are we going to pass into the night and be forgotten?"*

A week later I sat across from Marilyn sipping my coffee, listening to her tell about her evening with Emily. She described the boys they flirted with, who chased them in their car, and how they ditched them by cutting through an alley. It was good to hear young people having so much fun. Eric was secretive about his social life, but Marilyn covered every little detail of their night on the town.

Changing the subject she said. "The other day one of my coworkers at the office asked me what I was working on. I told him about the book I was writing, and he asked if I was going to write an article on it for the paper."

I bristled at the thought of having my life exposed in the paper, of my interest in the new age movement, and my knowledge of spirits and unseen energies. I didn't want to get into a similar problem like Carolyn faced with the police. "What kind of article are you thinking about," I inquired?

"I don't know exactly." She saw the anxious look on my face and wanted to change the subject.

"You can write about meditation groups," I suggested. There are probably many different groups you can interview. Each group probably focuses on something different. Our group is into healing, vibration, energy, and spirit. Others might seek God through meditation. Groups are a way of socializing around a certain theme. I personally am not ready to have my name in the paper."

"I understand. I didn't mean to write about our conversations."

"That's a relief. For a moment I was concerned. I'm still searching to find myself. Until I know who I am, I want to stay away from public scrutiny."

Turning on her recorder she said, "Tell me more about your meditation group."

"Well, the group has been a good outlet for me socially. Every week we meet and there's always something new. Sometimes we have a guest, who has special abilities, but we have managed to stay a core group, and Carolyn feels better keeping it small and intimate.

One Thursday night we were sitting on the patio at Carolyn's house and Ouizi told us about her helping Charles with Uncle John's writings.

* * *

Ouizi said. "Charles wanted me to help him organize his Uncle John's writings. I arrived early the first morning letting myself in with the key he had given me. The house was not air conditioned, and I wanted to get the work done before it got too hot.

I went to the kitchen to make some tea. In the cupboard I found a dusty canister with a few tea bags left. It had probably not been opened since his Uncle disappeared. I boiled water in the tea kettle, filled my cup, and allowed it to brew. With the teacup in hand I made my way to the Uncle's office where I found piles of papers waiting to be organized.

There were stacks of paper everywhere. I tackled the first pile. Not having organized metaphysical files I wasn't sure how to begin. I thought if I read the first paragraph of each page I could sort them out by topic. The first paper clipped file was a bit musty and faded, but it was titled *Jethro*. Was he someone from the Bible, presently living, or a character? I would have to read more than the titles to get the messages. Another said *Conversation with Einstein* and another said *Abuse*. I decided on broad categories, science, religion, mind and so forth.

Charles told me his Uncle John had disappeared several years ago. The neighbors called him when they hadn't seen his uncle for several days. When he arrived he found Uncle John's car in the garage, lights on in the house, and food in the refrigerator but no Uncle. He needed an attorney to help him as the courts would not let him settle the estate without a death certificate. Without a dead body he had to wait 7 years, and was just now getting permission to sell the house.

After sorting a while I took a break because my eyes strain easily. I took off my glasses to rest them, and walked through the house to the back yard. Charles hadn't spent much time taking care of the yard. Weeds had taken over the flower beds. Vines needed trimming and the grass was burning up in the hot summer sun. It must have been a nurturing yard at one time.

Back in the office I continued classifying documents. I came across a letter addressed to Charles and wondered why it was among the writings. Curiously I opened it and read it not realizing it might be personal. I didn't understand all that was said in the letter. It left me confused and bewildered. It talked of mind travel, teleporting the body to another time, and was signed by someone named Kathryn. She must have been a close friend of his Uncle's. I folded the letter and put it back in the envelope as Charles walked in the front door. He had brought me some folders and boxes to help with the files. He asked how I was doing, and if I had made any head ways before seeing the letter in my hands."

"I found that letter on the kitchen workbench when I came to check on my uncle," he said. "It sounds preposterous. This woman said Uncle John disappeared. How can anyone just disappear? I don't know what to think. I didn't even know he had a lady friend. I thought I would take the letter to the meditation class where we could all discuss it. What do you think?"

"I think that is a good idea." "Have you made any headway?"

I pointed to a small stack I had made. "Can you give me some idea what your uncle's interests were? Maybe it'll give me clues as to how to classify these files. Several writings talk about universal laws. I have put them all in this pile, but that's as far as I've gotten."

"He had many interests, science, astronomy, religions, creation, esoteric writings and the evolution of the mind. He had been to the Mid East several times and spent long periods in meditation. I think he could mind travel. One paper I read talked about layered realities; another, the expansion and contraction of the universe."

"Here is one on mind travel," I said. "I always wanted to learn more about the workings of the mind. Maybe that's the clue to understanding how to organize these writings. Do you have a computer? It might be easier to organize them on a computer. I could title each one and give a brief outline of its contents. I can take notes and transfer them to my home computer unless you have a portable I can use."

"Yes, that's a good idea, but I would rather keep all the writings here for now. I'll get you a laptop computer to make your work easier." Then he mentioned. "Some of Uncle John's writings will be controversial as he was a free thinker. If we decide to publish them I'm sure some people will be offended."

"Well if that's the case they don't have to read them. They can't deprive us of our right to know," I said sarcastically.

He noticed me tensing up. "For a short slender woman you can be expressive behind those horn rimmed glasses."

We both laughed. "It might be good to take some of these papers to meditation. It might make some sense if we could discuss them. Maybe we could even get in touch with Uncle John's spirit," I said.

"I'll think about it. I've to get back to the office. See you later Ouizi," he said.

I worked a few more hours taking more notes before I left. Wanting to take some of the files with me I remembered Charles saying something about keeping everything in tact until the job was done, so I left empty handed."

* * *

Marilyn got up to straighten her skirt and hinted she wanted to go outside for a cigarette, pointing to the pack lying on the table. I nodded and we headed for the door. "There's a lot I have to learn. All these terms you mentioned, laws of the universe and mind travel. I can see organized religion trying to discourage people delving into it, yet it sounds like part of God's plan," she said, lighting her cigarette, and inhaling deeply.

"I know what you mean. Each religion has its dogma, the rules they want to live by, but it keeps them stuck in time with no room for growth. Everything is evolving just like the universe is ever expanding. Anything that doesn't expand eventually loses motion, and collapses in on itself. That will always be. It's like one of those universal laws. Mankind has to allow for it. If man didn't evolve we would not have cars, telephones, computers, and trips to the moon. We'd still be living in caves and walking on all fours. It's all part of God's plan."

"What you told me today gives me an idea for my article. Maybe the evolution of the mind is the next step for mankind, and maybe meditation groups are the beginning of a whole new way of thinking. I wonder if people could separate spirit from religion long enough to grasp the bigger picture, the evolution of man."

"Maybe you better stick with something simple," I suggested. "You don't want to turn your readers off in the first sentence."

"You're right. I can see why it's taking you so long to reach your goals.

There is so much uncharted territory."

"Charles has been keeping tight control on what he brings to meditation. I would like to read them, but some things may be beyond our ability to understand. If the public gets their hands on the documents, he thinks they will destroy them."

"I don't understand," she said.

"If they are made known before their time, these documents could undermine the very foundation of religions and governments. When people find out who they really are and their capabilities, organizations will have no way to control them. Can you see how this would affect the world? If a person can learn to disappear like Uncle John, how can you keep them in tow? You can't."

"Jim, I see what you mean, but it's exciting to think about. I guess that's why they call it science fiction. You can make a movie about it and get away with it, but when it can be scientifically proven it then becomes a different matter."

"Yes. You see what a mess society has made out of UFOs. They would put this in the same category."

"I better keep it simple." She sighed putting out her cigarette and brushing her hair out of her face. "See you next week?"

"I'll be here."

CHAPTER 7

*"When you open to wisdom the voice of where
you are spiritually, speaks through you."*

Each week at meditation, Charles told us more about Uncle John. I called him after I got home from work one evening. His wife, Betty, answered. He was out jogging with his son, Kevin. They jogged several times a week. When he returned my call I asked him if we could meet one evening. I wanted to know more about his Uncle, and we arranged to meet the following Tuesday evening at the Uncle's house. He was standing in the driveway when I arrived.

"It's good to see you," I said.

"Please forgive the way the yard looks. I didn't get a chance to mow it last weekend," he replied.

"No problem," I responded.

We entered the living room. He hadn't removed any of the furniture. He led the way thru the house volunteering information as if he were giving a tour. I was intrigued, hoping he would say something to pique my interest. "And, this is the office where Uncle John did all his writing," he said. "He wasn't very organized, and I didn't get anything out of his writings at first, but the more I read, the more I realized he must have been on to something.

The first night I came here was on a Friday. My wife stayed home to take care of the kids and I spent the night here alone. I was planning to clean out the house during the weekend. That night I felt uncomfortable sleeping in his bed. I tossed and turned all night.

Towards morning I dreamed I was in a bubble floating in space with some young people. A crack developed in the side of the bubble and I saw the Earth. I was concerned the children might fall through the crack. The bubble landed on a hill and as it skidded along we came to a ravine. I leaned to the left to balance the bubble so it wouldn't go over the edge. Then it hit something and I awoke without the faintest clue as to what I had dreamed. I shaved, showered, and went into the kitchen to see if there was anything to eat. I made some coffee, found some stale crackers, and set down to go through his notes. As the day progressed I remembered the dream, something about a bubble in outer space and children hurting from an accident. What did it all mean?

I finished cleaning out the desk drawers and started on the book case. Before I crated up any books I wanted to see if there were any I wanted to keep. I kept them separate and boxed the rest. In the corner of one shelf was a dusty stack of papers that had been sitting there for quite a while. I put them in the trash can and was carrying them to the garage when something told me to go through them first. There might be a valuable item in them. I fished them from the trash can, spread them on the kitchen table, and began going through them.

After checking each page I discarded it. Then one caught my eye, the title page of what appeared to be a book, written by my uncle. Neatly stacked under the title page was the rest of the manuscript, its pages soiled and creased as though someone had read them many times. I set it aside and finished going through the rest of the stack. In the evening I sat in a comfortable chair in the living room and began reading the manuscript. I read several pages when the word bubble caught my attention. Was this a coincidence or had I dreamed my Uncle's vision?

After a while I put the book down and went to bed. Although I wasn't really tired I wanted to lie down a while. With the light off in the bedroom I propped myself up against the headboard, legs crossed in front of me, and closed my eyes. I tried to clear my mind, but information from the book kept seeping into my brain. The bubble suddenly appeared and someone was standing beside it. It was Uncle

John. He motioned for me to come with him. There were no doors. We merged right through the wall into the bubble, then we sat down, and it quietly lifted off.

Where were we going? I felt uneasy. It moved into space and bumped something making me feel we might fall out. Then it corrected itself and we floated back to earth.

I looked out through the bubble wall as we approached. Everything changed, I didn't recognize anything. I saw children living in a cave, playing games, but nothing made sense to me. Why was my uncle showing me this? I opened my eyes and the vision ended.

This bubble vision apparently belonged to my Uncle. He was a space traveler. He didn't need any scientific equipment to travel, he used an imaginary bubble. Why was this vision so real? What about the children? In the vision they appeared healthy and happy, but in my dream they were injured and in need of consoling. I thought again about the manuscript. It had my uncle's name on it, but it seemed to be written from a spirit level.

I called my wife and told her I would be staying another night. I didn't want her to worry. She wanted to know if I would be home on Sunday to go jogging with Kevin. I told her that I would be home in the afternoon. I went out to the garage and retrieved the papers I had thrown away. I wanted to check them more thoroughly. Whatever energy was in this house was not to be disturbed until I had all the information.

I awoke about 4 to a motion in the room. As I opened my eyes John's image was beside the bed.

He spoke, "Soon you will understand the information I've given you. Before I left the planet I had the dream you experienced. In my space travels I went through a time warp. I landed on a planet I called Centura. The sands were eroding and the planet was dying. It would soon break up and drift into space. I told the inhabitants that I would take their children to another planet so their life might be spared. I took them in the bubble to Earth, and found a safe place for them to live but failed to keep my promise to their ancestors about watching over them. I became aware that something was wrong with them. In spirit I went back in time to where I left them, saw they were very ill, and their bloodline was in danger of dying out. I couldn't allow it to happen. I had made an agreement with their ancestors to watch over them. I called on my higher power to help me."

"I symbolically cut my finger and I touched their foreheads in a counter clockwise motion leaving a circle of blood. I also allowed a drop of blood to touch their tongues. The oldest male was first followed by the oldest female. Fourteen in all were administered to. The children hadn't built up immunity to the diseases on earth and had taken ill. I felt they needed a mix of my energy to heal their bodies and my thoughts to comfort them."

"If they were going to survive, they needed a leader, and I wanted them to be able to develop on their own with no outside interference. Again I asked my higher power for assistance. Instinctively I went to the oldest female. With my right hand I touched her stomach and visualized a seed planted deep within. She would have a child with my vibration pattern who would lead them in years to come."

"In spirit symbolism is the language. We communicate with symbols. I'm not bound by form and time. I can go anywhere I want. This way I can see far more than when I was physical. I can help to make the world a better place, and I'm not alone. There are other spirits assisting, watching over people and lands. As one evolves all things become possible."

He dissolved in front of my eyes leaving me confused. I know this sounds weird. If someone else had told me this story I wouldn't have believed it, but it actually happened to me in this house. What do you make of it, Jim?"

"It makes a good story, but I'm not quite ready to accept it as truth. I know a few things about spirit, but moving back and forth through time, and traveling to planets in a bubble sounds farfetched." I could see now why Charles needed help deciphering his Uncle's writings. Who would believe them? Even I needed further proof.

"I was afraid you wouldn't believe me Jim, but this actually happened to me, and it's not the only incidence. Carolyn said that Uncle John may have used a porthole somewhere in the house to travel through. Other weird things have happened here but I don't want to confuse you more than you are.

I want to sell this house, but Carolyn thinks I need a psychic to cleanse it first of my uncle's energy before it will sell. If I do that, I'm afraid I will lose valuable information. My Uncle wanted to make this planet a better place to live. I would like to take up where he left off, and it would be great to have someone to assist me. Would you be interested in working with me towards that end, Jim? I need to share it with someone, just to make sense of it. You have a logical mind."

"I have to think about it, Charles. Let me ponder it over and get back to you."

"Thanks a lot Jim," Charles said as we headed out the door.

Before departing I suggested to him that maybe the meditation group could meet at his Uncles house. With all of us together we might get more information. It would give us a chance to be more involved in his project. He thought that was a good idea.

The following day Carolyn called me to inquire if I would be interested in meeting at Charles' Uncle's house on Thursday. She had contacted the others and everyone had agreed.

Thursday evening we all arrived at his uncle's home around 6:30. Again Charles took everyone on a tour stopping in the office to tell the story of how he found his uncle's manuscript. We settled in the living room while he made some tea for us and found plates for our snacks. Sara and Ouizi sat on the couch and we chose soft chairs No one wanted to sit in Uncle John's favorite chair.

Carolyn began speaking. "Charles, you say Uncle John disappeared seven years ago and no one knows what happened?"

"Yes," he replied. "But the neighbors told me that they had seen him sitting in his chair in this room after he disappeared, although they didn't know the source of the light."

The group did their rituals of flowing energy and hands-on healing. Then, Charles turned off the lights leaving only the light on in the kitchen and we began our meditation. We didn't know what to expect, or if we might be visited by John.

Carolyn said something very quietly almost inaudible as though she was talking to someone, trying to interpret the actions of a spirit. She said it motioned for us to come with him, so we all mentally moved with it through a cave and down to a peaceful lake. By the dock floating in the water was a giant bubble. The spirit motioned for us to ride with him.

I couldn't see anything, and was relying on what Carolyn was describing. I felt an odd sensation like feeling weightless, floating in space, some bumpiness, and then nothing. Carolyn continued describing the event. She saw children, a cave, and wild animals all around. The kids were barely clad, but all appeared healthy. The bubble then went back into space to where a planet called Centrua had been. It was now a pile of rubble floating in space, and then we were back in the room.

We discussed the meditation and it seemed we were all in agreement with our findings. When it was over Charles got out several sets of papers for us to look at and discuss. At ten o'clock we took our leave, thanking him for holding the meditation.

As I was going out the door Charles handed me his uncle's favorite hat. It was an old tangerine cap with a large "B" on the front. "It stands for the Denver Broncos," he said. "I want you to have it. Put it on, see if it fits."

It did fit and I decided to honor him by wearing it home. Then I threw it in the closet with all my other hats. Funny thing though, I liked it and the following day I wore it when I walked in the park. It had good energy, sort of like when a kid wears his dad's clothes. I wanted to go hiking that weekend in the mountains, and would wear it then.

* * *

I found myself in the foothills on Saturday morning. It was September and the Aspens were starting to turn. What a wonderful day I thought, everything was just right, and me with my new hat. Wait until Edward sees his Dad wearing a Bronco's cap. That's sure to make him laugh.

The trail led upwards winding its way through the trees. The smells of fall were in the air, and mildly warm weather made everything perfect. I reached the summit in about an hour and stood gazing down the trail. There were a few people around, but it was still early. With the weather so nice, it would be crowded later.

I leaned against a large boulder gazing at the valley below feeling the warm sun on my face, closed my eyes for a while and had a vision. I saw John just as though he were standing in front of me. He didn't open his mouth, but I could hear his words. "Why do you doubt my existence? When you let go of your rigidity you too will be able to do all the things that now seem impossible. Take control of your destiny. Do you think everything stops when you pass into spirit? Only your body stops and your footprints don't show, but everything else continues. There are wonderful reasons for having a body, but there's far more freedom without it. You'll see."

John's words stuck with me all day. It gave me something to think about.

That evening after supper I called Charles and told him what had happened.

He said. "It was the hat."

"What do you mean, it was the hat?"

"I gave it to you because it had my uncle's energy in it. That's why you had the vision."

Then I understood. "You wanted me to have my own vision so that I would understand what John was all about."

"Now do you believe me, Jim?"

"It's making more sense to me. But just give me a few more days to think more about it. I'll see you next week."

* * *

Marilyn was listening to every word I said. I was glad she was recording it. "What a great story!" She said. "I really dig this spirit stuff! Do you have more?"

"Yes, I do. When I'm home in the evening and want to meditate, I put on my Broncos hat, close my eyes, and ask John a question. Then I watch where it takes me. He's not always there but when he is it's like having my own built in theater, watching movies unfolding in front of me."

"What a gift! I'm looking forward to next Saturday. I want to hear more."

I asked. "By the way, whatever happened to the guy you dated several weeks ago?"

"I don't know and do not care. You were right. He wasn't for me. Besides, Emily and I are having fun just hanging around. The next guy I date is going to have to be someone special."

"Are you and Emily going out again tonight?"

"Yes, we have found a club downtown to our liking. Several of my college friends go there."

"Have a good time. I have a dinner engagement tonight," I said.

She raised her eye brows as if to say, good for you, then said. "Good-bye, Jim," and left the coffee shop.

CHAPTER 8

"We live off the face of each other."

The first snow of the season fell destroying the last vestiges of fall. The beautiful autumn colors had all faded into drab discards lying on the ground. Marilyn was once again at her favorite table when I arrived at the coffee shop.

"Hello there," I said as our eyes met. "It looks like fall is almost over. What are you up to? You look absorbed in your work." She was scribbling in her notebook.

"I'm getting a head start on the article we discussed. My boss wants it ready for next week's publication."

"I'll get some coffee while you finish. Do you want anything from the counter?"

"No, I'm fine."

It seems the colder it gets the better coffee tastes. I sat down quietly and patiently waited for her to finish. Shortly she put down her pen and closed her notebook saying, "OK, now, I can greet you better. Good morning! How are you?"

"Good, in fact I'm feeling very well this morning. How's your article coming," I asked?

"Your suggestion was good. I interviewed several groups this week and have some really good stories. The more I hear the more convinced I am there's a lot of truth in what you are saying," she said. "I may end up doing a series on meditation and metaphysics."

"I'm glad it's working out for you. Here, I brought something for you to look at." I said handing her a pendulum. "I use this when I want answers to questions."

She examined it and handed it back. "Where did you get it?"

"At a metaphysical book store. They had a variety of them, various weights and sizes in their showcase. I picked out the one that seemed to work the best for me." It looked like a small top that kids would spin attached to a six inch gold chain. At the other end was a small brass knob for gripping.

"When I use the pendulum I hold the knob with two fingers so it can swing freely, and I don't try to influence its movement with my mind. I hold my hand up about eye level, and clear my mind so that a spirit guide can come through. Depending on the question, I call upon the one I think will give me the answer.

For most people when the pendulum swings back and forth that is a 'yes', if it swings in a circle it's a 'no'. Those are the two basic moves."

"It sounds easy, but what if it doesn't want to work," she asked?

"When I first started I got all sorts of movement, but it definitely moved. Occasionally it moved in reverse or from side to side. If I wasn't in a peaceful place I couldn't get a positive answer. Slowly I learned to interpret each move.

"How did you determine that?"

"I asked questions to which I knew the answers and watched how it moved, but then I felt it was subject to my energy. The real answers come when I don't know the answer, like, 'does the mind dwell outside the body' or, 'is a spirit trying to communicate with me'?"

"I see. Anything I should know before using it," she asked?

"Yes, your guides usually don't want to tell you the future because it's subject to change. Any event could change one's future. Also, if an answer can be interpreted either way the pendulum will swing in a 'yes' fashion. Example: You get up in the morning and ask. 'Should I go to work today?' The answer is 'yes', or you say, 'Should I stay home today?' Again, the answer is 'yes', because it doesn't matter either way. You could do either. Do you see what I mean?"

"Does it always work," she asked?

"There are times it didn't work for me, once for several weeks. I couldn't get a connection to spirit. Do you want to try it?" I asked, handing it to her.

"Yes," she held it up so it could swing freely. "What do I do first?"

"Clear you mind. Don't think of work or what you are going to do this evening. Empty your mind and let the pendulum swing freely. OK. Now ask a question where you know the answer."

She thought for a second. "Do I have on black slacks and a white blouse?" The pendulum slowly swung back and forth barely moving.

"That's a good sign. Usually the first time it doesn't do anything, but the more connected you are with spirit the more freely it will swing. Now ask a question you know is false."

"Is the sky green," she asked? Slowly it began to change course, like it couldn't make up its mind, then it made a definite circle.

"See, you can do it."

"Now, let me ask a question I don't know the answer to?" She sat quietly. I waited for her to speak out but apparently she didn't want me to hear what she was asking. About a minute later the pendulum swung back and forth indicating a 'yes'. She smiled and handed the pendulum back to me.

"I'll have to get one of those," she remarked. "I can get some good advice. There are a lot of things I could ask."

"Some day you will be able to converse with spirits without your pendulum, and most of the time it will be the spirits of loved ones like grandparents who are here to guide and protect you. All you have to do is ask who it is. Feel their energy as though they are physically with you, but if that doesn't work, say their names. When the right spirit is named you will know."

"That's great. I wonder why others don't use this."

"It's because most people view communicating with spirits as Voo-Doo and are afraid it would bring evil to them. In fact they think anything to do with spirits is evil. They don't think there are good spirits, or they don't believe in general."

"If all good spirits go to heaven, why would they stay behind anyway," she asked?

"Because it's normal to want to protect and guide the loved ones they leave behind. Often I feel Doris' energy near me. I know when she is around, and I ask her to help me make decisions that will be good for me." Changing the subject I asked. "Did I tell you about the night Charles brought the letter from John's friend to the meditation group?"

"No," she paused. "What was in the letter?"

* * *

One Thursday night Charles decided to bring the letter that Ouizi had found to read to the group. He wanted our opinion on what it meant. After we settled down in Carolyn's living room he took it out of the envelope and began to read.

> "*To Charles Martin,*
>
> *When you read this letter I will have departed this planet. My work here is also finished. I want you to do something for me. It is important to me and John, and I trust that you will succeed.*
>
> *In John's book case is a manuscript totally finished and ready to be published. It holds John's truths, his life's work. I want you to publish the book as it is written, and I also want to tell you what really happened.*
>
> *John had been in meditation far beyond what humans can sustain. I went to his house every evening to check on him. We knew he would be gone for quite a while as he had mentally journeyed to another solar system. One evening when I arrived I saw him sitting in his chair as usual. I went to the kitchen to fix some tea as I planned to meditate on his progress. When I came back into the living room he had vanished.*
>
> *We knew his mission would be risky. He had gone to a meeting in another solar system in an effort to find a solution to the deterioration of this planet. The*

planet had been steadily losing life force. I knew before he started his meditation there was a possibility he might not come back, and now I am leaving to find him. Charles, I want you to carry on your Uncle's work. John was remembering universal laws. Some are written down but much of it is stored in his computer. I hope you can access it. If you meditate on it more will come to you.

Thank you, it has been a pleasure knowing and loving your Uncle.

God Bless You.

Sincerely, Kathryn

We sat in silence for a moment pondering the letter. There were many questions left unanswered. "What does she mean she left to find him," I asked? Did he just vanish to another solar system?"

Charles said, "Uncle John had known this woman for a long time. I always wondered why they hadn't married. I met her on more than one occasion, but I never knew the true relationship." He paused for a moment, then, "I think they both ascended. I never heard of anyone other than Jesus ascending, but I guess anything is possible."

Carolyn was the next to speak. "If he has sacred information I'm not so sure it should be published. In the hands of the wrong people it could be dangerous. Being able to time travel or to disappear and reappear somewhere else, especially on another planet would be alright for highly developed souls, but can you imagine how the ability could be misused by criminals?"

"That's not all he could do," Ouizi remarked. "He could journey into the future or back into the past, and change things that would affect the outcome of future generations."

"Do you think he could go to the beginning of time to see how life evolved on this planet," I asked? "It would be interesting to find out."

Sara was a little bewildered about such an idea. "I don't know about the beginning of time, and I'm not interested in moving back in time. I just want to stay firmly planted here."

"How are you coming with organizing John's writings?" I asked Ouizi. "It's a long process, but I'm almost done. We just need to decide what to do with them when we're finished. Should we publish them, put them in a library, or hide them from the public?"

"She's right," Charles said. "When it's finished I may just put them all in a box and store them somewhere. I am reading the manuscript that was mentioned in the letter. Kathryn wanted me to publish it as written. The book can be read on several levels. Those who don't understand what it involves will just read it for the story, and those who have open minds will get much more out of it. It needs to be published, but I'm concerned that the world isn't ready for it. There are some things in the book that have the potential to be dangerous in the wrong hands like Carolyn mentioned."

"I would like to have a chance to read it," I said. "I'm fascinated by any knowledge on this subject. I'm sure some people will find it boring, and will put the book down after the first chapter. Others will think it's the work of the devil, but that's the way it goes."

"Did you ever find out what really happened to Kathryn," Carolyn asked?

"When I went to her apartment the landlady stopped me in the hallway. She said that Kathryn had given her the cat and her plants before she disappeared. She had a key. When she didn't see Kathryn for a few days she got concerned. In the apartment was a note telling her to give all her furniture to Salvation Army. The woman waited for thirty days thinking Kathryn would return. When she didn't return she called Salvation Army and had the apartment cleaned out."

"What are you going to do with your Uncle's house," Carolyn asked?

"I'm going to put it up for sale soon."

"When you do, I suggest it would be a good idea to have the house psychically cleaned of energy. Your Uncle's energy still lingers there, and it would help the house to sell if you cleanse it first," she said.

"Do you know anyone who can do that," Charles asked?

"Yes, I have a psychic realtor friend you can call. Give him my name and tell him what you need. He can handle it for you." She paused for a moment then said, "In fact, if none of you care, I will invite him to our next meditation so that everyone can meet him."

"That's a great idea. I wonder if Doris is haunting my house," I said jokingly. "Maybe he could give me some ideas about selling my house. I'm thinking of getting something smaller."

Charles said, "I want to call him tomorrow. My Uncle's home has been sitting idle too long."

Carolyn took out a pen, wrote down the name and phone number and handed it to him. "Here give him a call. I would like to be there when he goes through the house if you don't mind. I have cleaned spirits out of a few houses myself, and would like to see how he does his cleansing."

"Sure, I'll call you," Charles said. "Thanks."

"OK, let's meditate," Carolyn said as she turned down the lights and everyone got quiet. A hush came over the group as all relaxed and we were quiet for quite a while.

After the meditation we all had interesting revelations, even Sara. I think John was in our midst. In fact Carolyn mentioned she saw a masculine spirit behind Charles, and that she could feel his energy. Charles said that he felt his Uncles energy very strongly in the room.

Before we left I quietly took Charles aside asking him if I could also be present because I'd become fascinated by the spirit world and he agreed to have me there as well.

All night I thought about the letter wondering how much was true, and about going to John's home for the cleansing. It really fascinated me.

* * *

"What a story!" Marilyn said. "I'm glad the tape recorder was on. I can almost put this verbatim in our book. You know, I could write a book just on group meditations. They've been very revealing. By the way, what happened to John's computer?"

"It wouldn't boot up when Charles turned it on. He took it to a repair shop, but for some reason they couldn't retrieve any information. It was wiped clean. It's a good thing John printed it on paper, or it would've been totally destroyed."

"You mean even the disks were no good?"

"We couldn't find any disks. I don't think Uncle John knew how to save them to disks."

"We covered a lot today. Let's save some for next week," she suggested gathering her papers. "I have to be going. I have lots to do before tonight. Emily and I are going to the Club again, and I want to finish writing this article before then."

"Okay," I said politely getting up from the table. "Next week I'll tell you what happened the day I met the psychic realtor. Have a good time tonight."

CHAPTER 9

"When you hush a people you strengthen their voice."

The Saturday coffee breaks had become an important part of my routine. I enjoyed the interaction, the aroma of fresh brewed coffee on these frosty mornings, the wide variety of people of all ages, some with hangovers from the previous night's festivities, and others just wanting to enjoy a fresh brew before work. Whatever the reason, their being here helped me to understand why Marilyn had chosen this location for her people watching.

What I enjoyed most was the company of this young woman. She made me feel important. 'Each person in this shop has their own story,' she would say, and that's why she comes here, to record their stories. No matter how mundane a life seems, it's important for humanity to learn from it, and she wanted to hear my story.

Marilyn was again waiting for me when I arrived and was talking to a young man about her age. I didn't want to interfere, but when she saw me she motioned me over. "This is Darrel. He works in the book store next door. If you want to know about a particular book ask him."

"Good to meet you, Darrel," I said shaking his hand.

"It's a pleasure to meet you too, sir. I've never had the privilege of meeting an author in the process of writing a book about someone's life. I would like to read it when it's published," he said.

Turning to Marilyn, "That makes at least two sales, Darrel's and my Mother's." I tried not to laugh, but she caught the remark and smiled.

"Be positive," she said. "Your story's important. People will want to read it."

"I need to clock in," Darrel said. "It's been a pleasure meeting you both.

If I can help you find a book let me know." He was smiling as he left the coffee shop.

"You have a dry sense of humor, Jim, but in a way it's refreshing," she said. "Shall we get down to work?"

"Do you remember where I left off last week," I asked?

She looked at her notes. "You were talking about meeting a Realtor last week."

"Now I remember."

* * *

I meet Vincent the Realtor, at John's house. What an experience! Charles opened the door to a portly man in a bright sports coat with a loud tie. His eyes were so bright his whole face lit up. So jolly he'd make a good Santa. It immediately put us in a good mood.

"Good morning, I'm your local ghost buster," he said chuckling in an upbeat manner. Although it wasn't that funny, his voice radiated with humor. It made us all laugh. "Now, let me see, where is he hiding?" Again, there was more laughter.

"No, it's not that kind of problem," Carolyn remarked, referring to Charles' Uncle. "We don't think he's haunting the place. We're concerned that his energy would keep buyers from wanting the house."

"Oh, in that case let's just party," Vincent said moving his large frame around as though dancing.

We all liked him and his energy was contagious. "Are you always this humorous," I asked?

"No, I'm just getting started. I take after my Grandfather. He taught me everything I know."

As quickly as he had filled the room with laughter he quieted down. "I'm not always like this, but Carolyn told me I was in good company, so I didn't think anyone would mind if I acted myself. Usually when I get a call to psychically clean a house the people are fearful, and I try to lighten it up with humor. I hope I haven't offended anyone."

"No offense. My Uncle would have enjoyed your humor," Charles said. "What do we do first?"

"The first thing we do is check physical energy sources to see if any ley lines might be crossing the property. Ley lines are electromagnetic energy bands circling the planet. They can be narrow or wide, and they can cross each other at different angles." Vincent took out two long brass rods bent at right angles on one end. He held the bent ends in his hands so the straight ends could move freely back and forth in front of him. He began walking through the house. "If there are ley lines coming through the house, these dowsing rods will find them."

He checked all the rooms and in the master bedroom the rods started pulling together. He tested several locations in the room and then gave us his findings. "A ley line comes in through this wall, goes across the bed, and out at the window. In fact they crossed when he lay in bed. Energy would have hit his upper chest and head, and could have heightened his psychic ability. It also might have given him a stiff neck."

Although making sense I didn't know anything about ley lines. How could something you can't see affect a person's psyche?

Vincent explained further. "When a person is meditating or sleeping, excessive energy will affect the outcome."

He then walked to the back yard to see where the lines entered and exited the house. He crisscrossed the yard picking them up again at the perimeter of the property. He eyeballed the direction. In line of sight was a tree diseased at the trunk. "Energy from the ley line may have damaged this tree. I would cut it down and put something else in its place, maybe a statue or just leave it in grass."

Walking to the side yard where the lines came out of the house he saw a sickly shrub. The branches were knobby and full of green mold. "Here is more damage," he said. "If it were my house I would pull this up also."

We were all surprised how something like a ley line could go undetected for such a long time. "No one thinks to check for ley lines when they buy a property. Almost every property has them. It's okay. Once you find them you can landscape around them."

Back in the house Vincent pulled a pendulum out of his pocket and repeated the same pattern. He found a vortex in the living room where John's favorite chair sat. Charles excitedly remarked. "What does that mean?"

Vincent laughed. "If you sat here long enough, you would feel empowered. This vortex draws energy out of the ground. Like sitting on a dome, without knowing why all of a sudden you would feel great because it gives your body a boost."

He continued checking the house. At the sliding door to the back yard Vincent's pendulum did a wide spiral. "Here is another vortex. See how the pendulum spins. This vortex is sucking energy down through it."

"The pendulum is spinning in the opposite direction for this vortex. Is that natural," I asked?

"Yes, it is. That is one way of knowing which way the energy is flowing," he said with a smile. Vincent did everything with flair. He was putting on a show and we were enjoying it.

With the pendulum in front of him, he continued walking through the house. When he got to Uncle John's office his pendulum stopped working. "This is unusual," he remarked. "Let me be alone in here for a few minutes."

We all took a break and went to the back porch. Charles offered us cans of pop and we stood there discussing our observations. A few minutes later Vincent joined us. He seemed to have mixed emotions. He wanted to smile but seemed confused. His face had a troubled look. We hadn't told him the room was where John's writings had been stored.

"I'm not sure how to say this. Sometimes there are no words to convey what one sees in spirit. I just have to use the words that best describe what I see and feel.

When I entered the door it was like I wasn't in the house. This may sound weird, but I don't think I was on the planet. I had moved through a doorway to another dimension. Everything physical disappeared, but there was light, and color, and words, and energy, and vibrations, all mixed together. If I'd been there longer I might have picked out one vibration and followed it. It was like a bunch of numbers bursting on a screen, as though each number had some significance. If I could spend time in there alone I'm sure I could write volumes, but few would be able to read it. I would have to make up words to describe it and that would dilute its meaning. It's confusing. I've never come up against such a collage of information."

"If it were possible I would take a picture of what I saw so that I could go there again." Turning to Charles, "You want to sell the house so I'm going to have to shut this porthole down. No one will want to buy this house with an open pathway to the universe. It would scare them too much, make them feel uncomfortable. I wouldn't want to sleep in that room. I don't know where I would end up."

* * *

I saw Marilyn squirm with that last statement. "This is scary and exciting.

I don't want to miss any of it," she said, checking her tape recorder.

"I'm glad you are open minded. Many people would think it was evil and turn it off, not wanting to think about it. Do you want me to continue?"

"Yes, by all means, finish your story.

* * *

"This is serious" Charles said. "Ouizi sat in that room for hours at a time. I'm glad she didn't sleep on the job. She might have disappeared. Can you fix it?"

"Yes, it'll take a while"

"What do you want us to do," I asked?

"I'm not sure what it will take. I need to find out how far the opening extends. The energy must be changed, disassembled, or softened, eventually the opening will close."

"Will it affect Uncle John's writings?"

"It might. If you read his writings while in this room you would gain far greater knowledge than reading them elsewhere. Once the porthole is closed it'll be twice as difficult to understand."

"Is there any other way to contain it," Charles asked?

Vincent thought for a while. "Yes, but it's dangerous. Quite risky, but I can do it."

"What's that," Carolyn asked? She was really excited as she had similar episodes while cleaning out other houses, and wanted to know what surprise Vincent had in store for us.

"Do you have anything that Uncle John wrote with you?" "I have his book in my car," Charles volunteered.

"Okay, maybe I can shrink this dimension so it fits into the book. Then the porthole can be accessed through it. You can store the book, but don't put it anywhere in your house. Hide it somewhere so that it won't interfere with the lives of those around you. If you want to preserve this, it can be done. The dimension can reside in the book."

"Okay, I'll go get it." In a moment Charles was back with the book. Vincent took it with both hands and waltzed into the room alone. We started to follow but he shook his head.

"Please stay out. I need to do this alone. I don't want any of this energy being absorbed by any of you when I shrink it."

He was gone a half hour. Time was running out for me. I needed to get back to the office.

"It's done," Vincent exclaimed coming out of the room. "Check for yourself."

Just in time, I thought. We walked into the room. He'd opened the window to allow fresh air in. It felt bright and cheerful, not the dark musty smell that had been there earlier.

"Does anyone have a box in their car," he asked?

"I have one in my trunk," I said.

"Would you get it," Vincent asked? "I don't want any energy rubbing off this book." I got the box. He put the book in it and handed it to Charles. "I suggest you bury it where it won't disintegrate until the right person comes along who knows how to use its power."

Symbolically showing finality he rubbed his hands saying. "My work is done."

Carolyn said. "Would you tell me what you did?" She was curious about the process, in case she needed to perform the ritual, but Vincent was sort of mysterious about his art and wouldn't disclose it.

"Some other time," he said laughing as if to say it was a secret.

I spoke up. "Carolyn, if you don't mind I'd like to invite Vincent to our meditations. Would it be alright if he came?"

"Yes, Vincent, will you come?"

"If I can fit it in my schedule," he said thrilled that he could be in a group that accepted him for his psychic ability.

We said our farewells and I headed to my office.

* * *

Vincent came to our next meditation, again, eyes sparkling and full of laughter. Before the meditation we sat at Carolyn's dining table giving him our full attention. He told us ghost stories that scared us one minute and made us laugh the next. Ouizi comes off shy, but when she gets going she too bubbles over with laughter. The two hit it off well together. Vincent told a story that was so hilarious she raised her hand knocking off her thick glasses sending them across the room. I laughed so hard my stomach hurt. "Laughter is good medicine," he said.

When we settled in the living room to meditate I asked him about John's house. "Were there any ghosts in his house?"

"I prefer to call them spirits. The word ghost has a negative connotation. When there are spirits in a house I can tell because they don't stay in one place. They move around. I can also sense their emotional energy, usually one of fear, sadness or loneliness. I take my kit of incense, potions and candles where ever I go. I'm well prepared. The spirit is there because of something that hasn't been completed. In many cases they aren't aware they have died."

Vincent continued. "The incident in John's office was a new experience for me. I've been thinking about it ever since. It goes beyond my expertise. All I could think of was closing the opening. It felt like I went into another dimension totally foreign to me, and I couldn't absorb it. It was more than a spirit thing. It was sort of a reservoir of universal knowledge layered one on the other. It would take years, lifetimes for anyone to assimilate it, if ever. I'm glad I could fold the vision into the book otherwise it would have been lost, a real shame to lose such knowledge. In the right hands that book is the most valuable thing on this planet."

Ouizi asked. "What is the most difficult thing you have to deal with, Vincent?"

"An evil spirit," he answered. "It takes a lot of energy to get an evil spirit to leave. Sometimes it refuses and I have to go back a second and third time. Removing a spirit that doesn't want to leave wears me out. It takes me days to regain my strength.

I became aware of a spirit, not evil, in a home I had listed for sale. She was the original owner. The house was almost a hundred years old. I convinced her to go with me into the light. When we arrived we were in a meadow the most beautiful pastel green I'd ever seen. Normally the vision is a bright white and spirits that appear are darker shadows. When her friends saw her they clustered around her. It was a fine reunion. Spirits generally stay once they are with their loved ones, but Charlotte, that was her name, was back in the house the next time I held an open house.

A curious thing, she didn't like children. I told her she could stay in the home if the buyer's didn't mind, but they may have children. I noticed couples with children who came through the house left quickly. When singles or a couple without children came through they lingered asking lots of questions.

After the open house I meditated to find out why she came back. Then I saw it. There was an image in the parlor by the bay window of a casket holding her deceased husband. She wasn't going to vacate the home while his energy remained in the living room.

I made a mental image of the coffin and kept that image in my mind as I drove to the closest cemetery. Once there I mentally placed the coffin in the ground, saying to her that he was now at peace. The next day I had reason to go back into the house and she was gone.

The house had been on the market for several months, but it sold within a week after this incident. It had been built by her husband at the turn of the century which explained why the energy remained there. She loved the home very much. It was a very unique home, a one of a kind."

"Do you have to clean out many homes," I asked?

"I check every home for foreign energy. Usually candles, incense, fresh air, light, or water is all that is needed. Sometimes I use music. One time the sellers had found their aunt dead on the family room floor. She had been there several days. It smelled and it left a permanent energy pattern. The carpet had to be replaced.

As a realtor one has to use every means available to sell a home and often that involves psychically cleaning it."

He turned to Sara mentioning that she had an Indian spirit behind her and something about it being her grandfather.

"He is with me all the time. I think I was his favorite granddaughter," she exclaimed.

"Where did you get your psychic ability," Carolyn asked Vincent?

"It came from my Grandfather. He was psychic and when I was young he caught me talking to spirits. Instead of discouraging me, we had three way conversations with them. He encouraged me to keep the connection, saying that most spirits were good and not to fear them. Fear draws evil. If I sensed fear I was to laugh out loud, and that would scare them away. It's the same in the physical world. If you can laugh at fear it goes away."

I had never thought of it that way but I knew he was right. As I drove home that night I couldn't help but be amazed how Vincent could light up a room with his eyes and his smile. I wished I had that ability.

* * *

Marilyn was so engrossed in the story she didn't even desire a cigarette break. She had literally been on the edge of her chair all morning. "You are talking about spirits and I'm going to a Halloween party at the Club tonight. Emily and I are dressing up as southern belles."

"You'll make a great southern belle. When I was younger I went to my share of Halloween parties. Tonight I have a date. We are probably going to a movie. You have a good time."

"I will. See you next Saturday." She said walking out the door.

CHAPTER 10

"Words from your lips disclose the love in your heart".

I was visited by a stray dog this chilly overcast morning. She was in the yard when I woke up. Feeling sorry for her I put a pan of water out on the doorstep so that she might have a drink. How she got over the fence into the yard I didn't know, unless someone left the back gate open. I was going to be late for my Saturday meeting with Marilyn and left the house.

"Sorry I'm late, I had an early morning visitor who needed some attention. It took more time than I thought."

"That's alright," she said. "I've been people watching as usual."

I turned to see who she was watching and noticed a young man getting coffee at the counter. "Your watching is improving?"

"Yes, but after being dumped last month I'm not ready to venture back into the water," she replied. "But a girl can still look."

"No harm in that," I said turning towards the counter. "Let me get a cup of coffee and we can begin. I want to tell you about the park."

I bought a cup of house blend coffee and two donuts thinking Marilyn might want one and sat down. "Have you had breakfast? Here is a donut."

"Thanks, I have something for you," she said with a big smile. She opened her folder, took out an article, and handed it to me. "It's my article on meditations, a half page of print. It even has my picture."

"Marilyn, this is great! I knew you could do it. May I take this home to read?"

"Sure, that copy is for you."

"Thanks, how did your Halloween Party go last week?"

"Emily and I dressed up in our costumes and we went to the Club about ten o'clock. The place was packed and almost everyone had on costumes. It was lots of fun. We stayed late. I drank a little too much. Luckily Emily didn't drink and she drove me home about 3 AM. Maybe you should go there sometime. There are people your age and you'd enjoy it."

"I don't stay out late any more. I'm usually in bed by the time the bar crowd arrives. I've had a few dates lately with a friend," I said. "We're kind of comfortable together."

"I didn't know you were seeing someone. Is it serious," she asked?

"It could be, but right now we are just getting to know each other. Only time will tell. Have I mentioned anything to you about Carolyn and hiking in the park," I asked?

As on cue, Marilyn clicked on her tape recorder, picked up a pen and was ready for another story.

I relaxed for a moment, took a deep breath and settled back in my chair.

Then I began.

* * *

"One day Carolyn mentioned that she wanted to go hiking in the mountains. I knew a park not too far from town and suggested we go there. The following Saturday I picked her up around ten and we headed into the mountains.

It was a bright sunny morning. When we arrived at the park we put on our gear and hiked up the path mostly in silence towards the first peak."

She said. "I feel spirits in this park. Do you know anything about the ground here? Is it sacred ground?"

"Not that I know of," I commented.

"Well it feels sacred, as though Indians might have lived here or used it for rituals."

Up ahead was an aspen grove and smack in the center a bunch of boulders. "Let's sit here a while," she suggested.

We climbed up on the boulders and sat facing the valley below. The sun was directly in front of us. It felt good.

"Did I ever tell you that I have a Native American guide," she mentioned. "I call him, Straight Arrow. Whenever I want some clarity on a problem I'm having or I lose something, I call on Straight Arrow to help me. If you don't mind I would like to meditate a few minutes to get in touch with him. I'm curious about this area and the energy I feel."

"I don't mind, I feel like closing my eyes anyway." The sun was warming me up and relaxing me. "Go ahead, I'll meditate too."

We meditated for twenty minutes before she spoke. "Straight Arrow said this is holy ground. Indians came here to talk peace. At various times they also lived here. Hunting was good and the evergreens provided shelter from the wind and the hot sun. He is pointing to a clearing down below us. That's where they lived."

She was silent for a few more minutes. "He says you lived with them." "You mean I was a Native American in a previous life," I asked?

"Wait a minute." She paused. "No, you were a white boy on a wagon train with your parents and sister heading west. The wagon train was attacked and all were killed except you. You survived by hiding behind a boulder. After the tribe who attacked left, you wandered several miles until you were found by the tribe that lived here. You lived with them for a few years, but couldn't adapt to their way of living. You died young. There was another Indian, a boy your age who found you. He was called something Bear, like Running Bear. You were good friends. He was a happy boy who could run like the wind. You barely kept up with him. Straight Arrow says that Running Bear will come to you if you meditate and think of him running with the wind."

"Very interesting," I commented. "Is there anything else he can tell us about the area?"

"No, but he says you were drawn to this place because it was familiar to you before and your spirit remembers it." She then became quiet and returned to her meditation.

I had often wondered why I picked one location over another. I'd been to several state parks, but always liked this one the best. In the last few years I had learned how to decipher one spirit from another by their energy. Now I would try to use that ability to feel the energy of Running Bear. I got quiet picturing a young Indian boy who was running and laughing, but didn't feel any spirit energy. I decided to try later in the quiet of my home.

Carolyn finished her meditation and stood up. "Let's go down the path to the clearing below to see if I can get any more information on how the tribe lived," she suggested.

"Okay by me."

"Here it is," she said after we walked for about 10 minutes. The clearing was encircled by tall stately evergreens. We tried to put our arms around one, standing on each side, but the trunks were so big we could not touch hands.

"Can you feel the energy of this tree," Carolyn asked?

"Yes, but I think it's only coming from one side, the side facing the sun," I remarked. I could feel energy pouring out of the tree on the sunny side. Checking other evergreens the energy was being drained off on the sunny side as well. I'd never noticed that before.

"Yes," she replied. "The sun draws energy from all living things. At night it is replenished from the soil where the sun deposits energy. I think this is where the tribe built their campfire. I sense them sitting in a circle around it."

"I wonder what happened to the tribe," I said.

"There are still many Native American spirits here," she said. "Their spirits are at peace. It's as though they never left and continue to nourish the area."

I thought that if I could go back in time they would appear. Their energy had probably been absorbed by the earth, rocks, and trees. That was probably why Carolyn could feel it. As we stood there quietly, two elk ventured through the clearing stopping occasionally to take a bite of grass. We were afraid to move for fear we would destroy the moment.

* * *

My coffee had gotten cold and I wanted another cup to warm me up. "Do you think it will snow?" I asked Marilyn.

"I hope not, Emily and I are going back to the Club tonight," she remarked.

"Did I tell you why I was late," I asked? "Not really, just something about a visitor."

"A dog ventured into my yard this morning. She was shivering and acted like she was lost. I wonder if she will be there when I get home. It would be nice to have another dog. It had been a while. This dog reminds me of a previous dog I had." I said.

* * *

"A friend gave me a small passive male dog. He made a good companion, but he was old and died after a couple years. I was fond of him and he would follow me around the yard watering every plant and bush he could raise his leg to. One day when I was working in the front yard he wandered off. I walked to the neighbors thinking they might have seen him, but they had not. Then I got in the car, drove up, and down the streets trying to find him. Finally I decided to use my intuition."

"I went home and sat in a chair on the patio. I meditated for a few minutes thinking of Running Bear for the first time. Surely he was a hunter and knew how to find things. This time he appeared in my meditation. I heard. 'With the eyes of an eagle, go in the direction of the wind.'

I got out of the chair visioning I was an eagle circling over head looking for him. I could see him coming out from a yard down the street. I left the house jogged in that direction, turning the corner and gazing down the street. There he was sniffing the plants along the side of a house.

I had never used my sixth sense like that before and was amazed it worked so well. I thanked Running Bear for helping me. It gave me a sense of being able to rely on my intuition. In fact, it connected me to my higher self. I had learned that I could rely on the unseen to assist me. It was like a light going on, and I wasn't alone on this planet. There were forces I could use to make life easier. After that I needn't worry when my dog wondered off. I knew I would be able to find him."

* * *

"That's an interesting story. But getting back to you and Carolyn, has there been any romantic interest between you two," Marilyn asked?

"We hike in the mountains often and have had discussions about the future. Whenever we meet we hug each other. Same as when we leave. Once I kissed her on the cheek and could feel her tense up. Later I thought about it and decided I needed a friend more than a romantic interest, so we're just good friends. Did I tell you about the time Carolyn healed me?"

"No you haven't. I'd like to hear it, after a cigarette, if you don't mind." She said changing positions on her chair.

She went outside and I got another cup of coffee.

* * *

It was in December the year after Doris died. I was feeling lonely and sorry for myself. Christmas was approaching, and Doris was not there to enjoy it with me. I came down with a sore throat and chest congestion. I have always gotten over colds quickly, but this time it lingered. People say the first Christmas after you lose a love one is the hardest. It certainly was. January and February passed, but still I could feel this tightness in my chest. I was constantly coughing and the cold just didn't want to go away. It was affecting my work. With tax season approaching the office was getting busy.

In March I asked Carolyn if she wanted to go hiking. It was warming up and we had a few nice days. She agreed and that Saturday we headed for the park where we had first gone. We hiked to the boulders and sat down facing the sun. There was still some snow under the trees and on the north side of large rocks. I told her about my cold problem.

She suggested I sit there quietly while she used her pendulum to find the source of my blockage. Soon she said. "You have blocked energy in your chest and also in your throat."

"What are you feeling right now," she asked? "I am feeling sad, lonely, and congested." "Who do you see when you feel those things?"

I hadn't thought about it. "I see Doris, her illness and empathize with her pain."

"Well, no wonder you're all congested. You are taking on her energy. When you empathize with another person you take on their energy. Her issue is not your issue, and you can release it any time you want."

"How can I do that?"

"Talk to her, and tell her you are sorry she is gone. Apologize for anything that you may have done to offend her and ask for forgiveness. Then suggest it's time for her to go into the light. If she can't find the light take her to it. You can't continually keep thinking about her. You have to let her go. Now take a deep breath."

Carolyn put one hand on my back, the other on my chest and said. "Inhale slowly and force it out quickly. Feel her energy leave your body."

"We did this procedure several times. Each time I pictured the blocked energy loosening up and going out with the breath. Eventually it was all gone."

I told her. "If I had known it was this easy I would have done this in December."

"Illness is nothing more than blocked energy not allowing life force to flow. Next time you feel ill, visualize the area of pain and you'll see what's going on."

What a revelation! Again I was amazed, I was learning so much about the unseen world.

I told Mom the next day when I picked her up for church about my healing expecting her to be as excited as I was. Her response was, "God heals in mysterious ways."

She never acknowledged the possibility I could heal or be healed. We each have our own beliefs and must allow others theirs. I was learning it wasn't right for me to impose my beliefs on others.

A few months later Carolyn mentioned to me that Sara had come to her saying her doctor had discovered an ovarian cyst that needed immediate attention. She was afraid she would have to be operated on. Carolyn took her to the park to an area that had a vortex. It was beside a line of boulders similar in size to the ones we sat on. She used her pendulum to find the energy blockage and did a healing similar to the one she did on me, except she allowed the vortex to draw out the blocked energy. The next week when Sara went back to the doctor he couldn't find any trace of the cyst and was surprised. Had he misdiagnosed?

* * *

"Now, that is quite a story. I'm sure the medical profession wouldn't want their patients knowing how to heal themselves. The American Medical Association would try to put a stop to it quickly."

"Yes, it's something one doesn't tell everyone about. Do you think it would be safe to mention it in the book," I asked?

She replied. "I'll have to think about that for a while. Whatever happened to John's house?"

"It sold quickly. Charles moved all the writings to his home, and I helped him bury the box in the field behind the house since Vincent said not to put them anywhere the energy could be contaminated. He hasn't published anything yet.

Marilyn, there is another incident that involves John that came from an unusual source. I think you might want to hear about it if you still have time this morning?"

"I'm in no hurry today. Let me take another cigarette break and I'll come right back," she said.

I went to the counter and ordered two house coffees and took them back to our table. Shortly she returned, thanked me for the coffee and clicked on her recorder.

CHAPTER 11

"A spirit does not evolve until it completes its creation."

Mom had a by-pass operation and was recuperating in her condominium. I spent a lot of time with her, along with her friends from the other units in her building. One day several women were with her when I arrived, so I thought I would take a stroll around the building. Sitting in the lobby was an elderly gentleman gazing out into the courtyard. I went over and introduced myself. We started talking and I told him a little about my life, about my wife dying, and about my still being able to be with her in spirit. He motioned for me to sit next to him, and in a childlike manner he proceeded to tell me his story.

"I see and hear spirits too," he said touching me on the arm. "Sometimes they tell me what to do, but I have learned not to listen to them.

When I was a young man I had lots of energy and got into trouble often. Other kids would dare me and I would take them up on it. It cost me broken arms, bruises, busted lips, and sore muscles. There was a part of me that kept rebelling and would not give me peace. I was struggling with myself and sometimes found myself arguing out loud with someone who wasn't there. I had to be doing something all the time to keep from hearing this other voice. It often got me into trouble. My dad would come down hard on me. He was quite a disciplinarian, but it didn't seem to do any good. I was arrested, kicked out of school, and known around the town as a trouble maker.

One day my Mom took me to a doctor who prescribed pills to calm me down. They helped. The other voice stopped interfering with my mind. I was able to sit still in class so the teacher wouldn't holler at me. Without them I would not have graduated.

When I was a teenager I stole cigarettes and booze, often getting into fights and going home drunk. Dad took away my privileges many times but it just made me defiant. When I graduated I left home. I dropped out of society, joined the peace movement, smoked marijuana, and tried harder substances too. I was part of all that. I got married but it didn't last a year. This other voice never stopped interfering. When I was high I was relaxed and at peace with it. Jobs came and went, as I wasn't dependable enough for the boss. I was dying inside and didn't know where to turn.

One day in desperation I went to see a psychiatrist. I told her my problems and about this spirit that was always interfering with my mind. She never offered any opinions, just let me talk. After several sessions I asked her what was wrong with me. She suggested a few things, saying that I had a split personality, which I already knew. I wanted to find a way to get rid of it so I could get some peace in my life. I kept pressing her for answers and one day she took me to see a psychic named John. Since I believed this was spirit related she thought he might be able to help me.

We sat in John's parlor and I told him my story. He held my hand and got real quiet as though going into a trance. Then he told me what he saw reliving the events. John said. 'When you were conceived your parents didn't want any more children. It was the Depression and they couldn't afford another mouth to feed, but your Mom got pregnant anyway, and an abortion wasn't an alternative. That was the physical side of what happened, but in spirit there were two spirits waiting to be born to your parents. One was from the lineage of your Mother, the other from your Father. Ordinarily there should have been twins so that each spirit could have had its own body, but there was only one fetus. The spirits knew there wouldn't be another opportunity for them, and both spirits opted to inhabit one body. They each wanted their own voice causing a rift between them as to who would be the dominant one. The stronger personality won out and matured. The other, still a child in many ways, needed to experience its childhood. Hence, a conflict occurred.'

I asked what I could do to make peace. Could I send the other spirit away or find a way to permanently keep it subdued? John indicated it wouldn't work. 'Both have a right to be in this body. The voice you hear is the other spirit expressing itself.'

He also said. 'If a spirit entered the body after birth it could be sent away, but when spirits were born at the same time they both had a right to experience through their physical body. You will have to learn to live with and make peace with your other spirit. Both of you have to be allowed to express yourselves and experience life to its fullest. After all that is why you are here.' He said. 'If you stop fighting you can live in peace. There was nothing wrong with allowing the other to take over once in a while.'

After that meeting I felt much better inside, and I allowed more space for my other half. I tried telling some of my friends about this incident but they didn't believe me. I swore to never tell anyone else. I just didn't feel comfortable sharing my feelings with others especially those who didn't understand spirits.

Then one day I met a woman and fell in love again. I got up the courage to tell her about my other personality. It didn't seem to bother her. In fact we even joked about it and she allowed this younger spirit room to express itself. After we were married I asked if she wanted children but she said that my inner child was enough for her to handle. We spent forty-two years together until she died.

When you mentioned the spirit of your wife I knew it was safe to tell you, that you would understand."

I thanked him for sharing his story and went back upstairs to my Mother's unit.

* * *

Marilyn said. "Let me get this straight. This man had two spirits in his body, and he couldn't have an exorcist remove one of them?"

"They both had a right to be here. They entered at the time of birth and knew there wouldn't be another chance to be a born of these parents. Neither one wanted to pass up the experience. If one decided to leave for another reason it would be their right, otherwise they would live together until they died."

"I'm confused. You say there are spirits waiting to be born, and they can be the lineage of either parent," she said.

"Yes, spirits evolve together to complete agreements, and they move from one lifetime to another playing different rolls until the energy of whatever agreement they have is dissolved. In this case one spirit was from each parent."

"I will have to think about this for a while."

"There are also many spirits with no connections wanting to take human form. They sometimes slip in ahead of a waiting spirit. All deserve a right to experience human life, but they are not part of the family's spiritual bloodline. This hijacking of a body results in abortions, love/hate relationships with parents, and abandonment of children.

I don't know whether this will confuse you or not, but there's one more thing I want to add about spirits."

"Go ahead. I'm getting this on tape so I can listen to it until I understand it."

I continued. "When I talk about spirits the subject is foreign to most humans. People tend to fear the spirit world and don't want to go there. Eventually one gets comfortable with the idea that spirits are a natural part of life and always have been. We are all spirits with a human body. If you think about it for a minute, it's far more fearful to be in physical form than to be in spirit. No one can really hurt a spirit. Only the body can be hurt, but the spirit can't experience this physical side unless it has a body.

Anyway what I want to tell you is that there are times that spirits split apart and become two as in the case of identical twins. After they are born they start having different experiences and eventually have their own personality. In their next lifetime they may be born individually but usually within the same family because their energy is still similar."

"You are right. I'm going to have to listen to that explanation many times to understand it," she replied.

"It's possible for the original spirit to have many counterparts alive at the same time, and it's possible for them to meet one another. Talk about joy when that happens. I think that's what being a soul-mate is about."

Jim continued. "I met someone whom I thought was one of my spirit twins. Our birthdays were the same, so were our interests, thoughts, hobbies, and beliefs. I couldn't believe how much alike we were. The only difference was that he was born in a different country and had different experiences. Hence his background gave his story a different flavor.

Marilyn, I think I've confused you enough for one day. It's getting late and I have a date to get ready for. Are we meeting again next week?"

Clicking off her recorder she said. "Sure, have a pleasant week. I have another article to write for the paper that's going to take a lot of research. I'll probably be spending most of the week at the library," she said gathering her papers and stuffing them into her briefcase. "See you later."

CHAPTER 12

"Events last as long as they take, and not a moment longer."

Rain turned to snow on Friday night. As I backed out of the garage Saturday morning my car slid on the ice. The temperature had dropped during the night but the sun was out, and I hoped it would melt the unwanted precipitation. I drove carefully trying to avoid the slippery spots and arrived at the coffee shop ahead of Marilyn. There were few customers. I made my way to the counter, ordered my coffee, and sat down at a table near the wall. Our favorite spot by the window was taken by two young men with spiked hair who wore baggy clothes. They were reading the sport pages of the morning paper. I aimlessly leafed through a newspaper someone had left while I waited for Marilyn. A half hour passed before she finally arrived. A makeup covered black eye distorted a face deprived of a good night's sleep. She walked cautiously as though experiencing pain. I stood to greet her.

"What happened to you," I exclaimed? My first thought was that she had been assaulted.

"It's a long story, and I don't want to waste valuable time," she replied. "I'm getting a late start and I have to leave early."

She appeared to need some emotional support. "Sit down and I'll get you some coffee." Returning to the table with a steamy cup of brew I said. "Today is going to be your day. My story can wait. I want to know what happened to you."

She let out a big sigh. "I'd rather not talk about it." She hesitated a moment, then spoke, "Emily and I had an accident last night.

We were going home and she slid on the ice. The car in front of us braked, and she tried to avoid hitting them. We slid to the left and the car behind us rammed the driver's side. I only have a few bruises, but she's in the hospital," Marilyn said with tears in her eyes.

"I'm so sorry. Is she hurt badly?"

"She broke her left arm. Her head hit the steering wheel and cracked the wind shield."

"Will Emily be in the hospital long," I asked?

"No, the doctor said she would be released in a day or two. She is awake and in observation right now. She doesn't seem to have suffered any major brain trauma. I'm going to see her when I leave here. I feel pretty shook up, and have been smoking like a steam engine. In fact I need one right now. Would you mind if I went outside for a smoke?"

"No, I'll go with you."

We grabbed out coats, picked up our coffee cups, and walked outside where the sun was shining. She lit up a cigarette and continued. "We were both taken to the hospital. My injuries were minor so I was released, but I didn't have a way home. I called Mom and she met me there. We spent most of the night talking about what happened which is why I got a late start today. I wish my dad was here. He would've known what to do."

"Well, I'm here for you. Can I do anything to help make you feel better?" "Yes, tell me why life is so hard," she asked?

"That's a tall order. I think it's because as humans we are blind to the future. We see only the events that unfold today and aren't privy to what happens tomorrow. We don't know what lies ahead. We can only respond to what happens today. If we could look at the greater picture we would find a purpose behind every happening. There are no accidents. Everything has a purpose, and we just need to find out what it is. As you get older you learn how to avoid some of these events. When you are my age and look back you can see a pattern. There's a greater design for your life and each event is important in shaping it.

Let me tell you about my son's accident last summer.

* * *

Eric graduated from college the previous month and was despondent because of all the resumes he sent out that went unanswered. He wanted a job in astronomy, but wasn't having any luck. He was afraid he would have to take a job outside his chosen field. He held off moving from the campus area because a job might open out of town, and he didn't want to move twice.

I suggested he take a trip into the mountains for the weekend, do some camping and hiking to clear his mind. He took his telescope, the new camera my Mom and I had given him for graduation, and headed west.

I got a call from the County Sheriff's office late that evening. Eric swerved to avoid hitting an elk. He went down an embankment, rolled over, and hit a tree. Fortunately a car behind him saw what happened and called for help. He was airlifted to St. Joseph's Hospital in Denver. He had broken bones and internal bleeding. Mom and I went to see him every day until he was released and then he spent several weeks recuperating at home. He finally fully recovered, thank heavens. I don't think I could've handled another death in the family.

* * *

Marilyn was silent for a moment, then, she spoke. "Jim, you lost your wife and then this happens to your son. I don't know what it's like losing family members. To lose my mother would hurt terribly. It makes my accident seem trivial. Thank you for putting my accident into prospective. I'll get over my bruises and black eye, and Emily will probably be fine after her arm heals. What's it like to lose someone close to you?"

Her manner changed from victim to survivor. She straightened up and a smile brought sparkle back to her face. The spiked hair guys left as we went back in, and we were able to sit at our favorite table.

"It depends on whether it's after a long illness or a quick death. When it's a long illness like Doris', you have time to complete issues and do those things that cement relationships. There's no greater sense of fulfillment than when you have the privilege of taking care of a loved one whose days are numbered. You can never seem to do enough. You make each minute count. The love you feel has no boundaries. When she was in pain we prayed that God in His mercy would help us find peace. On the good days we rejoiced. I found myself doing things like bathing and feeding her that I would never have thought of doing before. We laughed and we cried together, and when I thought I could cry no more, she died. Although I was thoroughly worn out after the funeral there was a great sense of peace. My Mother and sons were there, and we comforted each other.

Then the mourning took over. I tried to keep busy so I wouldn't think of her, but when I was idle I would see her everywhere, and hear her voice, yet I knew I would never be able to touch her again. As the days passed the hurt became less.

If the death is quick and you haven't had time to complete issues it's more difficult. You ask God to give you just a few more minutes so you can tell them how much you love them, but it too late. Your differences no longer matter, when you feel robbed of an opportunity. I think it takes longer to get over the passing as all the mourning is done after their death. I don't know which one is easier to endure.

From both you learn to allow people to be themselves, and not to get caught up in things that don't matter. Never let the sun go down on your anger. You may never get another chance to clear the air and to make peace. Never carry around excess baggage, and live each day as though it may be your last."

"That's sage advice," she said. "This makes me wish my dad was here. I miss having him around. I hardly know him."

"Maybe the day will come when he will visit you, but until then, I would be proud to take his place. Changing the subject, "How long have you known Emily," I asked?

"We were in high school together. Best friends, whenever one of us got into trouble we both did. We would hang around after school and on weekends, we played hooky together, and got caught smoking together. I had forgotten all about her until several weeks ago when you told me to call someone to take my mind off the creep. She came to my rescue just like she always did in high school."

"Friends like her last a lifetime. When you are my age they will still be close to you. It's because you have worked out issues with them, and you feel comfortable with each other. Your secrets remain for a lifetime."

"Well, I really must be going. I want to get to the hospital."

We left the shop together and I walked her to her car. "Have a good week and keep warm," she said.

"I'll try." I said and closed her car door. I hadn't told Marilyn the whole story about Eric's accident as I wasn't sure how she would take it. I didn't want to detract from her traumatic incident.

I left the store and headed home. The snow was almost gone and I was grateful for the sun's warmth.

I had a date tonight with Shirley and didn't want to drive on slippery roads. I had met her at the hospital when Eric had his accident. Over the last few months we had grown accustomed to each other, and I looked forward to my time with her as much as seeing Marilyn each Saturday. I finally had women in my life, and it felt good.

CHAPTER 13

"There are no accidents and no victims." Everything happens according to God's plan.

"How is Emily?" I asked, savoring my first cup of coffee. "Is she out of the hospital?" The shop was buzzing with young college students chatting over lattes. I was glad Marilyn always got here early so she could find a table.

"She's doing fine and was only in the hospital two days. Her arm will be in a cast for several weeks, but it's not slowing her down. She wants to go to the Club tonight, but I'll have to drive, which means no alcohol for me. I don't ever want to have another experience like last week."

"Good idea," I said, taking a sip of coffee. "Marilyn, I didn't tell you the whole story about Eric's accident last week."

"That's okay. I was in no condition to listen. Let me turn on the tape recorder."

* * *

My employer had built up a large clientele over the years and last spring I was kept very busy. After twenty years with the firm I had gotten tired of handling other people's taxes, and when the April 15th deadline came it was a relief. I was happy to finally get some time off.

I offered to let Eric have his reception at my house after graduation, but he preferred to have it at his apartment. It was small and I didn't know where he would seat everyone, but then again I had nothing to do but show up. I went to the astronomy store, found a camera for his telescope, took it home, and wrapped it.

Graduation Day came. Mom and I went to the stadium together for the ceremony. We watched him being handed his diploma, and were proud of his accomplishments. Afterwards we congratulated him and headed for his apartment. It wasn't long before the place was crammed with college kids. Not feeling comfortable with the noise and close quarters, we gave him our gifts, stayed only a short time and said our good-byes. I was happy Eric had so many friends. It reminded me of the days when I was in college.

Mom and I went to dinner, at one of our favorite places, a small Italian restaurant in the neighborhood. During the meal she leaned forward and mentioned, "Now that the kids are gone maybe it's time you started dating again."

"Mom, I was thinking the same thing. I spend far too much time at home. My only real outlet is my meditation group," I said. "Thank heavens for them. I would be lonely without them. I thought that Carolyn and I might get together, but she didn't seem inclined. I talked to her about it but she politely said she was happy being single. She said one shouldn't have two psychics in the same household and I took it to mean friends only." I wanted to meet someone who aroused passion in me and made me feel alive. Maybe I'm too particular, but Doris was a hard act to follow.

* * *

The following weekend Eric went to church with us. Mom was happy to see him. She makes such a fuss over him, and he loves her attention.

"How is your job hunting," I asked him?

Eric's mood turned somber. "Not very well, Dad. I thought the university would take me on, but they don't have an opening. I don't want to move out of town and to leave you and Grandma. I'm thinking about going back to school in the fall and taking up related subjects to enhance my knowledge of astronomy and science.

I thought about taking quantum physics and reality theory, and maybe going into research."

"That's good. I'd love for you to stay in Denver, but you have to make your own life no matter where it takes you," his Grandmother said.

"Yes, Grandma. You're right. If something exciting comes along in another city I'll give it a lot of thought," he remarked.

I spoke up, "Electro-magnetic energy and its effect in the universe has always interested me. I personally would like to know more about your studies, and would be happy if you shared your findings with me. These topics require years of study though. Scientific theory constantly changes as new findings and theories are always evolving."

"I know, Dad, and if I get on at a university I can continue my research."

I suggested. "Take a drive into the mountains to clear your mind. It always works for me?"

"That's not a bad idea. Maybe I'll go this weekend." He said, as his mood visibly changed."

"Is your car able to get you there and back safely? You can take mine if you want." I was concerned that his car might break down leaving him stranded.

"Thanks for the offer, but I'll be just fine. My car got a tune up a few months ago."

Before we parted he again expressed concern about not having a job. I had helped him financially through college, and he felt embarrassed asking for more money. He wanted to be on his own. I just wanted him to be happy. I said. "You are too concerned about getting a job, Eric. You have your whole life ahead of you, and are only young once. Take your trip and enjoy the scenery. Relax and you will get a different perspective on things."

I tried to put a positive spin on his situation so that he would feel good about himself. I didn't want him to worry, although I was concerned about the finances. His going to college had drained my resources, and it would take some time to recover. Still he was my son and I wouldn't have it any other way. I was concerned however, and hoped that he would be alright.

The following Friday it was clear skies and 85 degrees. The leaves on the trees had matured to their full brilliance and flowering plants had committed themselves to God's glory. I drove home from work with the windows down enjoying every breath of fresh air, just happy to be alive. Later, while watching the late nightly news the phone rang. It was either a wrong number or something was wrong. It was the Jefferson County Sheriff. "Is this Jim Roberts," the voice inquired?

"Yes." I said. Something was definitely wrong.

"Your son has had an automobile accident and has been airlifted to St. Joseph's Hospital in Denver."

My heart skipped a beat and a hundred thoughts entered my mind. "How did it happen? Is he alright," I asked?

"You may want to go the hospital. I don't know his condition. He hit a tree. Fortunately he was wearing his safety belt," the sheriff remarked.

My heart sank. "Thank you for calling me, officer." I said as I hung up.

I thought for a moment then called Carolyn. "I'm going to need your help tonight. My son has been in a car accident. He's at St. Joseph's Hospital. Can you meet me there?"

"Yes, I will be there as soon as I can," she answered. "Is he in bad condition?"

"The sheriff just said I should go to the hospital," I replied.

I headed downtown to St. Joseph's. Over and over again, trying to convince myself, I said. "He'll be alright. Even without an air bag surely he couldn't be that bad."

Edward, his brother, was already in the waiting room when I arrived. The sheriff had also called him. "He's in surgery Dad," Edward said as I entered the room, but the look on his face was grave.

"Is he alright," I inquired?

"I don't know. He's been in surgery for some time," he replied. Just then Carolyn came through the door.

"I got here as quickly as I could. How is he," she asked? "We don't know. He's still in surgery"

Shortly the door opened and a nurse came into the room, asking for the family of Eric Roberts. She came over to talk to us saying. "Your son has been wheeled into recovery. You may see him but only for a few minutes. Come with me." She showed us to his bed in the recovery room. He looked so helpless, laying there, his head and chest bandaged. His left arm was in a cast up to his shoulder. Face bruised, his right eye was black and blue. I felt sad for him and wanted to cry.

"Dad, he's not so bad. It could've been worse," Edward said, trying to make us feel better. Ever since Doris died he felt he needed to be the pillar in the family, since I could barely handle the events around her death. Once again I was having a hard time staying in control and Edward noticed.

"He'll be just fine. He's young, and will bounce back quickly," he said. "I need to leave. I have to get some sleep. Morning comes early for me. If you hear anything or if anything changes, call me." He placed a hand on Eric's shoulder for a moment, then turned and left the room.

"Carolyn, thank you for coming tonight, for being there for Eric and me.

You are always there and ready to help out where needed."

"That's what friends are for," she responded. "As a psychic and healer I feel an obligation to help my friends in time of need. I know you would do the same for you me. You have proven it."

"Well, anyway, thank you," I said as an orderly approached. He told us they had found a bed for Eric in intensive care on the fifth floor. Carolyn and I waited in the hall for a few minutes while they moved him. Then, we took the elevator to the fifth floor ICU.

We sat near the nurse's station waiting for what seemed an eternity. Finally a nurse said. "You may see him now, but please only stay a few minutes. He needs his rest." I noticed the name on her badge read, Shirley.

"Thank you, Shirley," I said. We went into the room and were relieved that Eric had the room to himself. Carolyn and I planned to run healing energy through him and wanted privacy.

She and I stood on opposite sides of the bed. She was flowing energy with her hands and mentioned blockages in various areas. She moved her hands slowly sending energy to the injured areas. I followed her lead and moved my hands on my side of him. We were just getting a good start when the nurse came in.

"You will have to leave now," she said, observing what we were doing. "Can we have just a few more minutes," Carolyn asked?

"Okay, but don't stay too long."

We continued for a few more minutes then, Carolyn drew back her hands saying. "We should leave. It's getting late. He needs to rest and to allow the natural healing process to do its job."

She had barely finished speaking when something went wrong. The equipment started going off. The nurses rushed into the room, one of them hollered. "Someone call the doctor. He's going into shock."

Carolyn and I were ushered out of the room as the doctor came in. We stood in the hallway fearing the worst. It seemed like an eternity before the doctor came out, but when he did, he looked at us and said. "Don't stay too long. He needs his rest."

The nurses seemed confused. The alarms had gone off, but now they were questioning whether an emergency had existed. I looked at Carolyn and smiled. "May we stay a few more minutes?" I asked barely able to control my emotions.

"Sure, only a few," the nurse nodded and they all left the room.

Carolyn stayed so cool and collected. I felt emotionally upset and she acted as though it was routine. She put her hands back on him. With one hand on his head, she put the other over his heart.

I followed her lead, but thoughts were running through my mind. This can't by happening, Eric is too young. His whole life is ahead of him. He can't die. He's my son.

Then my thinking pattern changed. Wait a minute. People don't die until they are ready. That's what I was taught in meditation class. Surely Eric wasn't ready to go. He had too much to live for. I became positive.

Carolyn said. "We need to stretch time. If we can be alone with him a little longer running energy through his body maybe we can stabilize him." It seemed an eternity. Time slowed as I moved my hands in rhythm with hers.

The silence was deafening in the room. Carolyn was busy concentrating on her work. A voice within me said. 'Why are you so upset? He's not dead. Only his body stopped functioning. He is not dead until he decides to leave his body. Do whatever Carolyn tells you to do.' I knew that voice was correct. It made good sense.

Looking up to heaven visualizing the master of the universe I thought, 'Father, if it's Eric's desire to stay here put divine light into our hands that he be healed.' I silently prayed feeling life force energy flow. It felt right.

Then, another thought entered my mind and suddenly I felt the presence of angels in the room, the same feeling I had when my wife died. Had they come to take his spirit? I saw Eric with his mother and held my breath. Then he slowly turned around and headed towards me, moved right through me and was gone.

Carolyn was slowly inhaling and forcing air out through her mouth. I followed suit doing it in unison, just like we did in meditation class when we were clearing bad energy, I visualized a mountain setting with Eric alive and vibrant. Another voice in my head was directing me on what to do. I was to create a probable future with him, alive and happy.

The door opened and nurse, Shirley peaked into the room. She saw what we were doing and went for help. A few minutes later she brought another nurse with her and they asked if they could help. I motioned to Shirley to stand opposite of me, and for the other nurse to hold Eric's feet. Shirley put her palms under his back and I put mine on his chest. We all breathed in and out together as though we were one. Carolyn still had her hands under his head.

I mentioned. "Let's visualize him alive and vibrant as though no accident occurred." Carolyn nodded her approval. I had learned that a person could recreate their future anytime they chose by changing the energy patterns in their mind.

We continued for a while visualizing and feeling light going through our hands, but it didn't seem to do much good. The voice in my head said. "Don't give up now. Your work isn't finished. Continue what you are doing."

Then to Eric I said, "Come back it's not your time," and I began singing a cheery tune. Everyone joined in singing words of encouragement to him as though we were having a party in his honor. In fact we really got into it and it lifted our spirits. Then one of the nurses noticed a twitch in his fingers and she let out a gasp. The room fell silent. I felt a shallow chest movement then another. His eyes slowly opened. Nurse Shirley placed an oxygen mask on his face.

We were all so excited, everyone wanted to talk at once. I stayed by his side stroking his head and thanking the universe for giving him back to me. Carolyn was moving her hands over his body, checking for any more energy blockages. Watching her hands you could tell where the trauma was.

"Where am I," Eric haltingly whispered?

Looking down at him I said. "You are in St Joseph's hospital. You had a car accident."

"The last thing I remember I was driving up the hill. A deer jumped out in front of me. I hope I missed him."

"Apparently you lost control and your car hit a tree. You were airlifted to here. It was a close call but you are going to be just fine. We're happy to have you back among us."

Shirley explained that even though the hospital didn't approve of this type of healing some nurses had learned the art of hands-on-healing anyway. Then she said. "Let him get some rest now." I thanked them for helping us.

"Eric, I'll be back here tomorrow," I said and we left the room.

I was grateful to Carolyn for her support. She knew exactly what needed to be done. We had brought him out of his coma, and I wondered if the nurses would tell anyone or keep what happened, a secret.

I showed Carolyn to her car thanking her again for being there for us. She was such a good friend, so caring and true. I respected her desire to not have a more permanent relationship, but we were closer than any other woman I had ever known except my wife.

Getting in her car she gave me a warning. "It's important to be careful not to impose your will on another. One has to live with the consequences of their actions. If Eric doesn't gain all his mental faculties, you may have to take care of him the rest of his life. It has to be his will to live, and you might be keeping him here against his will."

I hadn't thought I might be imposing my will on him, but then again I may have. I would now have to continue to be positive on his healing. Then I remembered a saying from the Bible. 'Not my will but Thy will be done,' and I understood why the angels were there for him.

Carolyn interrupted my reverie. "You faced the cloud of fear again, didn't you?"

"Yes, I wasn't going to let it take my son. I had to go through it. I had no other choice."

"I saw resistant energy and you moving through it," she said getting into her car. "You were brave. You didn't hesitate and I'm proud of you." I thanked her and closed her car door then walked to mine.

It was late when I got home. I would call Edward and Mom in the morning. At least for now Eric was stabilized and awake. I was tired and needed sleep.

The next morning I awoke from a dream, and tried to recall as much as I could. An angel was saying. "You have no right to change destiny. What is done is done. He made his choice and determined it was his time to go."

"He made no such choice." I said to the angel. "When he stopped breathing he thought it was his time, but it wasn't his choice. If I hear him say he wants to die I won't interfere, but if he says I want to live, he will live."

Then the angel replied. "We empathize with people and we are there for them. We guide them and help them in their transition."

I said. "As it should be, but do you think it's alright for anyone to determine the destiny of another? Isn't it their choice? Do you think it's the destiny of this planet to have wars, crime, killings and famines? I don't believe God wants man to suffer in this manner. I don't think He wants us to keep this planet in darkness. Where is the hope we are to have? You are here to protect and guide us, and take us home when we are ready. Don't be so willing to take us while we still have another breath. We don't want to be controlled by others. We are going to take destiny into our hands. We are going to take responsibility for ourselves and recognize the God-force within us."

Where did all that information come from? I felt powerful. Surely it must have been someone else talking. I wrote down as much as I could so I wouldn't forget it. I wanted to share it with my meditation group.

I was now wide awake and decided to get up. 'When humanity first began there was a need to send someone to nurture man. Angels played an important role then and still do, but as man evolved it was necessary for him to assert his divine right, and take his place beside his Father, nurturing and ruling the planet together. Man must be equal partners with angels and other spirits in this endeavor.'

I called Mom that morning to let her know about Eric's accident and that he was at St. Joseph's Hospital. She was upset and I told her I would keep her informed. If she wanted to visit Eric we could, but I didn't want to tell her what transpired. She would not have understood.

She went with me to the hospital that afternoon and we took flowers. Eric had improved dramatically, but it would be a few more days before he would be taken off oxygen. He still had an IV and a tube draining blood from his chest, but his color was back.

When Mom went to the restroom Eric said to me. "I've been depressed, Dad. Nothing seemed to go the way I intended. I wanted a teaching position at the school when I graduated. My professor said he could get me on, but later said there were no positions available. Also, I'm still mourning on the passing of my Mother, and I miss her terribly. When I was in my coma I thought this was my time to check out, but your energy kept pulling me back."

"Carolyn and I performed a healing ceremony on you, son, but we didn't interfere. We can't heal you, but we can set the stage by keeping your energy flowing until you were ready to come back into your body. During a person's life there are, opportunities for one to pass, but time will not pass away until all things are completed. I knew your work wasn't finished. It has barely begun. You haven't done what you came here to do. If you intend to go you will have another opportunity. I can't force you to stay against your will. It would create bad karma for both of us."

I silently thanked the universe for giving him back.

He touched his chest and a pained expression appeared on his face. "My chest hurts when I breathe. The Doctor says I broke three ribs. One of them punctured my lung and I was bleeding internally."

"The universe was providing you a way out. In your depression you created an opening and the universe was fulfilling your wish."

Mom came back in the room. Shirley came in the room again insisting Eric needed to rest. I wanted to speak to her anyway so we excused ourselves and went into the hall. "Shirley, you know we didn't heal Eric. We just supplied the energy so he could heal himself. I don't want anyone to think a miraculous healing took place. It could cause a problem for all of us."

Shirley replied. "His heart did stop beating. I checked the monitor after you left. It definitely showed no heart beat. Whatever you did worked, but I won't tell anyone."

I went home thinking I should take a few days off. I let Edward know how Eric was doing but didn't tell him what had happened. He planned to visit him that evening.

That night I meditated for an hour affirming that Eric would recover quickly until negative thoughts came to mind about my wife's passing. All of a sudden I sensed a dark swirling energy around me. It wouldn't overtake me this time. I put up a shield and waited to see what would happen. Before long a voice said to me. "You can't do this. I rule this planet. I determine who lives and who dies."

I knew this to be the Evil One, this dark swirling mass of energy. This was the cloud I had feared all my life. This time I observed it without taking it on, and now I would be free of it once and for all. "I no longer believe in you." I said. "You cause destruction and create victims. Through fear you make people feel they have no control over their destiny. I know you exist, and there will always be those who believe in you. They give you their power, but you will have no power over me, and you will have no power over Eric. Be gone."

The Evil One argued. "It's unnatural that you should bring him back to life."

"It's unnatural that man should die before he completes his life's work, I replied. "If Jesus had a son who died he would certainly have brought him back to life."

"You can't do this. Humanity can't know they have power over life and death." The energy in my mind became intense. The colors of red and purple were swirling. Had it been anyone else they might have trembled in fear, but not me, not this time. Nothing was going to cause me to change my new belief. I lost my wife to her belief that someone or something controlled her destiny. I wasn't going to also lose my son if he wanted to stay. No way!

Again I said. "You have no power over me. My life and my death are my decision. It's time others know they control their destiny, and I shall tell them. For each of us it's our own decision." It left and I lit some candles, and focused my mind on a peaceful scene. I was amazed how strong I was becoming in my convictions. Another voice in my head said. "Well done".

On Sunday after church Mom and I went to see Eric. She took him a get well card and box of candy. She loved pampering him as he loved pampering her. When the two of them were alone they acted like a couple, and I sometimes wondered if Eric might have been my dad reincarnated.

Her visit did him a lot of good. She started calling him every day, and he improved steadily. In no time Eric was able to leave the hospital.

He came to stay at the house until he fully recovered. I mentally stationed spirit sentries at the corners of my property to keep out any negative influences. It was a ritual I have done for some time, but I wanted to make extra sure Eric would stay positive. With him home it was like old times.

One evening I asked him what happened when he had died for that short period of time. His eyes lit up and he said, "Dad, I saw the path way home, and I saw Mother standing at the entrance. She was beautiful. Light was coming from behind her, and yet her face was also bright and her hair sparkled. She told me it wasn't my time, and I should go back to take care of you. Then I felt your energy pulling me back."

I didn't tell him I saw them together and him turning to come back. I did not think he would be ready to hear it.

A week later the university called to inquire if Eric had found a job. Apparently the professor who taught astronomy had taken ill and would be out for a semester. Would Eric fill in for him?

When I came home from work that night Eric's face was lit up like a Christmas tree. "Dad, I got a job. I'm going to teach astronomy at the university this fall. Not only that but I will be able to take the courses I need to work towards my doctorate."

I was pleased, "Eric I know that you will become one of the best teachers on the staff and they will want you to stay! This is great news! Let's celebrate!"

That night we dined out at the neighborhood Italian Restaurant, on pasta and wine. We had a great time. I don't remember the two of us ever laughing so much. Eric wasn't only my son; he was becoming my best friend as well.

The news about the job gave him a lot of energy and he moved back to his apartment near campus. I was once again at home alone.

* * *

Marilyn said. "Do you mean you actually healed him after he died, and you brought him back to life?"

"No, we made it possible for him to heal himself. It felt good to be a part of the process, and brought me great satisfaction."

"Every time we meet you have something new that just blows me away.

What's next," she exclaimed?

Laughing, "I don't know, but I'll think of something," I said, shrugging it off. "If you aren't rushed for time I have a story to tell you. Would you like another cup of coffee?"

"I'm not rushed, but I do need a cigarette break. Would you come outside with me for a few minutes?"

"Sure." I followed her out front and she lit up, sighing as the smoke dissipated into the frosty air.

She turned to me and asked. "What story do you want to tell me?"

"I want to tell you about my first date, the first one since Doris died."

Her eyes brightened. She flipped on the recorder hanging by her side, and I began.

CHAPTER 14

"People are spirits acting out their dreams."

Every time I went to the hospital Shirley was on duty and we would engage in good conversation. I hadn't actually dated anyone since my wife died. Maybe she would go out with me, keep me company and maybe more.

Shirley was forty-five years old, about five feet six inches tall and weighed 150 pounds. Grey showed through her auburn hair, and her figure was similar to Doris'. Caring and compassionate, she was intelligent and politely conversational. I had asked her at the hospital if I could call her, and she happily agreed, giving me her phone number.

I wanted her to have dinner with me at my home, but I felt a little awkward.

Eric had only been out of the hospital two weeks and was still recuperating, so I asked him if he would help me. At first he was apprehensive. It didn't feel right that his dad should be dating another woman.

"Eric, I'm still human and I get lonely for female company," I said. "Your Mom will always be part of me. I feel her energy every day, I see her in my dreams, but it's not the same. I need a woman around to talk to, and it's been so long I feel awkward dating. What if she wants to get friendly? I wouldn't know what to do. Will you come to dinner to keep me from making a fool of myself?"

Eric laughed at my awkwardness. He'd not seen this side of me before. He thought his Dad could do anything, but now he seemed so vulnerable. He couldn't handle a simple date. "Yes, Dad, I'll be happy to be there," he replied.

That night I lay in bed thinking of my wife. 'I thank God for having had you in my life, Doris. I couldn't imagine living without you, and thought I would die when you left. Not being able to see your face, your eyes, has been most difficult for me. I miss hearing your voice and smelling your fresh washed hair scented with apple blossoms. I miss touching you, and feeling you in my arms.'

As I thought these things the room lit up and Doris's spirit appeared. She told me she was at peace and asked me to forgive her for leaving me. I forgave her and asked that she forgive me for not wanting her to go. I told her how lonely I was and that I wanted to start seeing other women. She smiled to indicate it was okay.

The next day I called Shirley at the hospital. "Shirley, its Jim Martin. I'd like to invite you to dinner at my home one night soon. Eric will be there too if that's alright with you. What nights do you have off?"

"I have Friday and Saturday off this week." She replied. Would one of those work for you or is that too soon?"

"It's not too soon." I gave her my address then asked. "Do you need transportation?"

"No, I have a car. What time do you want me over?"

Saturday at six o'clock will be fine. Do you eat chicken? I was thinking of roasting one on the grill"

"That sounds great. I will bring a dessert and be there about six on Saturday. Thanks for the invitation, Jim. Bye."

All week I planned and cleaned. I pulled weeds and watered the lawn, making sure everything in the yard looked perfect. I cleaned off the deck and planned to eat outside if the weather permitted. It was July, but in Colorado one never knows when it will rain. I planned the menu several times and finally settled on one and on the type of wine to serve. I even cut flowers for the dining table.

Eric noticed me fussing around trying to make everything perfect. "Dad, everything looks just fine. Take it easy. There's nothing to be nervous about."

"I want everything to be perfect. I haven't had a date in so long."

"You still haven't. A date is two people. I'm here. This doesn't count," he said jokingly. His humor helped me relax.

Shirley arrived shortly with a strawberry-rhubarb pie in hand. I was happy that she accepted my invitation so we could get further acquainted.

"Come in. It's so good to see you," I said. "I'm happy to be here," she replied.

"Let me take the pie to the kitchen," I suggested. She followed me, saw Eric, and inquired how he was recovering from his accident.

Shortly, I showed her through the house to the back deck. Eric appeared with two glasses of wine then disappeared so we could talk.

The chicken had been roasting on the grill, and I checked to see if it needed basting. I didn't want it to dry out.

"Do you know much about new age thought," I inquired?

"You mean like healing, running energy and spirits?" Shirley said her eyes lighting up. Before I knew it I had forgotten all about my nervousness, and we were deeply engrossed in conversation.

Meanwhile Eric was becoming impatient. The chicken surely must be done. He brought the other dishes out from the kitchen as if to suggest it was time to eat. Without losing a beat Shirley and I kept talking. Eric removed the chicken from the grill, carved and served it.

Hey, you two," he said, raising his voice. "I would like to say a word of thanks for us being together tonight."

We looked at him in surprise, having forgotten anyone else was there. As soon as he was finished with the prayer, we started up again and talked through the whole meal. Eric was happy that we found so much to talk about and he sat silently eating, nodding his head in agreement from time to time, not fully understanding what we were talking about. He was interested in spirit things, but not to the degree we seemed to be. I bet he wondered why I needed him to break the ice.

When dinner was over Eric cleared the table and ask if we wanted anything else. Finally he was included in the conversation. Shirley said. "I hear you have accepted a teaching position at the university.

It was Eric's turn to talk. He finally felt part of the conversation. He told her of his good fortune and how he would be one of the youngest teachers on campus.

It started getting dark so we decided to adjourn to the den for pie and ice cream. Shirley cut and served the pie, while Eric piled on the ice cream. I made the coffee and we carried all of it to the den.

"This is the finest pie I have ever tasted, Shirley."

"I picked the rhubarb from the patch behind my town house. This time of year it is so juicy and fresh. The strawberries came from the neighborhood market," she said.

"Well, it's the best I have ever tasted," I remarked with a smile and Eric agreed.

Eric hung around waiting for Shirley to leave. I guess he didn't want me to make a fool of myself on my first date.

After they left I wished I had kissed her, but it felt awkward with Eric around. I went to bed that night with pleasant thoughts dreaming about the future, one with Shirley in it.

She called the next day to thank me for dinner and to see if I would like to have coffee on her next day off and I agreed.

We met the next Tuesday morning at a local coffee shop. She was waiting for me when I arrived. A good sign, I thought. She saw me enter and nodded. I bought a latte and sat down at her table. "Good morning, another beautiful day in Colorado," I said cheerily. She smiled in agreement.

We sat for a moment sipping our coffee and thinking to ourselves. I was wondering what might be the motivating force that made Shirley decide to become a nurse. "Why did you choose a medical profession?"

Shirley sat quietly for a moment formulating in her mind what she wanted to say, then she spoke as if it happened yesterday. "My Dad got sick when I was young. Mom told me to nurse him back to health and to pray for God to make him better. I would say to him, 'I want to make you better Daddy,' and he would motion for me to sit by him on the bed. He would tell me stories. No matter how sick he was he always had a story to tell me."

This went on for quite a while. I tried everything I could think of to make him better. Sometimes Mom would give me a hot washrag to put on his head which he liked. The sicker he got the more we prayed. One day the doctor came and told Mom he needed to go to the hospital. An ambulance came and took him, and I never saw him again. It hurt so much, I blamed myself because I couldn't make him better, and I blamed God for not making him well, but Mom said it wasn't my fault or God's fault. People die and become spirits. In fact she said if I tried real hard he would visit me. I could see him and feel him near me.

I tried every day for a long time, but nothing happened. Then one day when I was just sitting in my room I saw him. He even touched me. I was so happy I could finally see him again. After that I didn't care what anyone else said, I could see him. I would ask him questions and he would tell me answers. He said he would always watch over me.

That's why I became a nurse, to help others when they get sick. I grew up wanting to be a nurse. My Dad still comes to me on occasion. I'm so appreciative of having his spirit connection," she sighed.

"Next time he comes to you, ask him if he will bring others to you. Maybe you can establish a spiritual network to answer questions you might have," I suggested. "Maybe he'll bring spirits with medical skills who can direct you in healing people spiritually. I believe that even though spirits have given up their physical bodies it doesn't mean they have lost the talents they developed while on earth."

I told Shirley about our meditation group and about how much I had learned while participating in our Thursday meditations. She asked if she could attend one of the meetings, and I said I'd check with Carolyn.

There was a pause in the conversation. Shirley looked at her watch and said. "I should leave. I still have a lot to do today. I won't have another day off for a week."

We stood up and Shirley put out her arms as if to receive a hug. I didn't need a signal. I was happy to oblige. It was a warm caring hug, maybe a tad too long. "Let's do this again soon. I've enjoyed your company very much." We walked out the door together. She turned one way and I the other.

It must have been two weeks before I heard from Shirley again. One morning she called my office and said she would be off the following Thursday and wanted to go to the meditation.

Two weeks later on Thursday night Shirley came to Carolyn's home. I introduced her to everyone and we did our usual meditation ceremony. I think Sara talked about her mountain trip visiting the ruins of her ancestors. She told us about how the Indian Chiefs would make it rain. When I walked Shirley to her car she asked. "Do you really think we can cause it to rain?"

"Yes, I do, Shirley, but if more people knew they can affect the weather we could have a problem. Someone would always want something different. One has to be careful not to overdo it. Flooding is a terrible thing."

Shirley looked questioningly at me. "Surely you are kidding," she responded?

"When meditating on rain our energy goes into the ethers and combines with spirits who bring about change. It's their energy that brings a change in the weather. We only enhance the chances of it raining."

"I think I understand," she responded.

"Do you want to get together sometime soon," I asked? "Sure, give me a call on Sunday. I'm off that day," she said.

I got another hug and a peck on the cheek, then, I drove home with a smile on my face.

The next day I called Mom to see if she was going to church on Sunday. I wanted to know if she would be home in the afternoon because I wanted to bring Shirley over to meet her. "I'm so glad you called Jim," she said. "Eric stopped by this week to see me. He told me about his new job. I'm happy for him. He brought me a framed picture of a comet he photographed on his telescope, Hale-Bop I think he called it. I want to hang it above my mantle. Will you help me put it up?"

"Yes Mom, I'll help hang his picture." Pausing for a second, then, "Mom, do you think I've waited long enough since Doris's death to start dating? I've met a woman and would like to spend time with her. She works at St Joseph's Hospital. Do you think it's alright?

"You have met a girl, how wonderful," she said excitedly. "When do I get to meet her?"

"You've already met her Mom. She was the nurse at the hospital when Eric was there. She has Sunday off and I was thinking that maybe she'd like to go to church with us. What do you think?"

"She seemed nice, but I didn't talk with her much. I would like to know her better Jim, but you don't need my approval to date her. You can handle your personal life without asking me. If you like her, that's all that matters."

"But I want you to like her too Mom. Your opinion is important to me." "That is very kind of you. Just let me know what you have planned. If you want to go somewhere else with her instead of to church that's alright too."

"Thanks Mom, I'll call you later. You have a great day. Good bye." "Bye Jim."

I then called Shirley. She was still at home. I asked if she would like to meet my mother on Sunday and she agreed. I thought, 'Every time I talk to her I feel good the rest of the day. Could this be a sign of things to come?'

I wanted to get mom's approval before I proceeded with the relationship not that I needed it but I would feel better.

That evening I did a long meditation. I wanted to know about Shirley, to see if our energy was compatible. In my darkened living room, I let my thoughts play out to the point I was in a dream state. Then I ask my higher self if her energy was compatible, and if not what would cause me discomfort. She lived by herself for a long time and appeared to be a loner. Could she be accepting of someone else living in her space? She likes to read, take care of her cat, and has friends whom I have never met. Each one of these ideas had energy, most were compatible except the independence and other friends. I could meet her friends. That might give me a clue.

This thinking went on for a while and then my processing shifted. Some other influence began taking over. Maybe I wasn't acceptable to her. My fears were short lived as I pushed the negativity away.

On Sunday we all met for church and then went to brunch afterward. Mom and Shirley were so intent on getting to know each other that I hardly got a word in. I was pleased that they got along so well.

Mom had given her approval and ever since we have been seeing each other regularly on her days off. I feel very comfortable with her and have resolved my apprehension regarding my late wife. Things were going well with Shirley and me.

* * *

We had been standing out in the chilly air and I was cold. I was sure Marilyn was freezing.

"How did it feel to finally start dating again," she asked?

"It felt good. I've been dating Shirley ever since I met her at the hospital when Eric had his accident. In fact I have a date with her this evening. I'm sorry I kept you so long today, but I wanted to bring you up to date on my love life."

"I'm glad someone has a love life. I keep waiting."

"Well, someday the right man will come along for you, you'll see. I'll see you next week."

"See you then," she said as we started walking to our cars.

CHAPTER 15

"We are all angels choosing human form to experience the wonder of creation, and offering each experience back to the One who created us."

Saturday morning Marilyn was sitting at her table with papers strewed all over when I entered the coffee shop. She was preparing an article for the newspaper and notes were everywhere. She looked up and saw me standing there patiently waiting her acknowledgement.

"Good morning," I said. "How was your week?"

"I've been real busy. My job is keeping me hopping as you can see. Have a seat."

"OK." I helped her gather her papers, went to the counter to get a cup of coffee and sat down.

"I'm finding myself devoting more time to journalism and less to people watching. I miss it and am glad you are here. It gives me a diversion."

"I look forward to these Saturdays also." We talked for a few minutes then I asked? "Are you ready for me to tell you more of my life?"

"Yes. I'll click on the recorder."

* * *

One evening Shirley and I were planning to go out for dinner again at the restaurant down the street from her. We had been seeing quite a lot of each other lately. A surprise was waiting for me.

I arrived at her home about 6 o'clock. As she opened the door I smelled pasta. "Hello, I thought we were going out tonight. It smells like plans have changed."

"Yes, I thought it might be nice to spend the evening right here," Shirley said closing the door.

"If I had known I would have brought some wine."

"Too late, I already have some here. If you want, you can open the bottle," she said leading the way to the kitchen. It's here on the counter top and the glasses are in the cupboard above it."

I opened the wine as she stirred the sauce. "That smells great!" I said.

"I had today off and decided to cook for a change. I even made dessert, but it's just for you. As you can tell from my hips, I don't need any."

"Nonsense, you look just fine. You'll never hear me complain about your looks."

"Thank you, dinner is ready so why don't you sit down and I'll serve."

The meal was far better than any Italian restaurant I had been to, and the wine was perfect. "Where did you learn to cook like that?"

"My mom was Italian. She taught me how to cook all her secret recipes. She is gone now, but every time I cook Italian food it's like she's here in my kitchen."

"I guess all mothers and daughters excel in cooking their ethnic food.

You are no exception. This is the best Italian food I've ever tasted." "Thank you," she replied.

When we finished I helped her clear the table and we adjourned to the living room where a log was burning in the fireplace. I walked over to the fire to stoke it as she sat on the couch. Then I sat beside her.

"I could get used to this," I said. "Better be careful. Don't spoil me too much."

She laughed. "I just do what comes naturally. This feels good to me too. Would you want to watch some TV? There's a good movie on. I could show you my picture albums or we could play scrabble or cards."

"Maybe we could just sit here and watch the fire," I said putting my hand on her's. I leaned over and gave her a kiss on the cheek. She put her arm around mine, planting a big kiss on my lips, and we settled back to enjoy the fire.

"It had been a long time. I'd forgotten how it felt being this close to someone. This is great!"

She agreed. "Don't get too comfortable. I still have coffee and dessert to serve."

"If it's anything like your lasagna I may never want to leave."

"It was good, wasn't it? It was one of the first Italian dishes I learned to cook, after spaghetti, that is. By the way, if you want to stay all night it's alright with me, but you will be all alone. I still have to work."

"Tonight," I questioned, feeling let down. There was a pause in the conversation.

"I'm just kidding," she said with a smile. "You're welcome to stay the night if you like."

"I don't want to force myself on you," I said.

"Let me worry about that. Would you put another log on the fire?"

I got up and went to the fireplace thinking, 'It had been a long time. I hope I don't disappoint her.' She went to the kitchen and brought out dessert. The berry pie and ice cream hit the spot, and coffee topped off a perfect meal.

"Thank you so much for dinner. You are a marvelous cook. I'd highly recommend this restaurant. In fact, I'll come again, that is, if I'm invited."

We talked for several hours while the fire burned low, then she led me to the bedroom, turning out the lights as we went.

* * *

"That's a good story, Jim. I love romance, wish it were mine," Marilyn exclaimed. "When did this take place?"

"This happened two months ago, and it's ongoing."

"Well, I wish I could find a guy who would romance me. Emily and I enjoy each other's company, but it's not the same. It's been so long. Are there any guys who want me," she asked?

"You bet, and he'll be in your life sooner than you think. You watch," I replied.

# CHAPTER 16

'Maybe our solar system is no larger than an atom.'

Another Saturday, Marilyn and I sat at the table savoring our first cup of coffee. She had asked me if I would tell her about my philosophy of life when an argument broke out at the counter.

"I didn't order an espresso. I ordered a latte," a young man barked in an argumentative manner.

I'd seen him in the coffee shop on several occasions, kind of like how one notices a person who always speaks loudly, or who makes a fuss when there's an easier way of communicating.

"I know what I ordered," he shouted!

The clerk in a polite voice said, "I'll let you have it free if you want it?" "No, I ordered a latte," he insisted!

Without thinking I stood up and went to her rescue. Standing beside the irate young man I quietly suggested, "Maybe God wants you to have an espresso this morning."

"You stay out of this," his anger now focused on me.

I should have stayed out of it. Normally my first instinct is to fight back, but that wouldn't help anyone. The clerk was busily making a latte for him to calm him down. "Here you are, one latte coming up."

He grabbed his drink and sat at a table across from us. I turned towards Marilyn but then decided to approach his table. "May I apologize," I asked? "I didn't mean to upset you. I just wanted to tell you something that might make your day a little easier."

"What's that," he asked sardonically?

"Everyone wants what they want. Sometimes God wants something else for them, but they don't see it. They bulldoze their way through life with blinders on, never looking left or right. There may be a reason God wants you to have an espresso this morning. There may have been spiritual communication before you got here. You said one thing, she heard another. No one is wrong because there are no mistakes. Just think about it," I suggested.

As I turned to leave his table he said, "Thank you, I apologize."

"You are welcome." He got up from his table and went back to the clerk apologizing to her for making a scene. Then, I breathed a sigh of relief.

"Boy, he cut you down," Marilyn said. "I wasn't sure how you were going to handle it, but you did alright. I'm proud of you."

"Thanks. A person sees one reality at a time. It's hard for them to consider an alternative because this one seems so real. My peaceful reality could have changed to match his but I chose not to let it. If I wouldn't have apologized to him I would have eventually found myself fighting off his anger and destroying my day. I don't know what happened to him last night, but something triggered this behavior."

"Yes, but you were cool about it. I would have hit him."

"Then, you would have taken on his energy. Maybe God wanted him to have an espresso because it had more caffeine, or maybe it was just another opportunity for him to learn a lesson. Who knows?"

Marilyn spoke leading me back to her initial question. "This works with my initial question. What about your philosophy of life, Jim?"

Thinking for a moment before I spoke, and knowing the tape recorder was running, I wanted to say it so she could understand it. "I believe God dwells within the hearts of all living things. I believe the body is his sanctuary and we should treat each person in a dignified manner, even our enemies.

I asked myself. 'If I were God, would I react this way, would I treat anyone without respect? Would I treat myself without respect?'

Marilyn, I want everyone to understand that we aren't victims living on an angry planet hoping to attain salvation when we die.

We are God creatures helping each other. We each experience things differently, for instance anger. Before it will disappear it has to be experienced every conceivable way, and whenever it comes up we have to decide how to manage it.

There are no two of us that look the same; there never will be, because each of us has different experiences. I believe we are spirits in human form, and this form is only the suit of clothes we wear that allows us to be treated the way we are treated. The energy we take on, anger, happy, sad, loving, active and passive attracts those who will match and enhance that energy. Anger doesn't generally draw peaceful energy to it. It draws more anger. That is why I couldn't allow that young man to change my energy pattern. Normally I would have just left the room, however his energy is in this room and affects all of us. I wanted to diffuse it so that we could have an enjoyable morning."

"I'm beginning to understand," she said.

Just then the young man came to our table saying, "I'm sorry I snapped at you this morning."

"That's okay," I said. "I know you didn't mean it." He nodded to Marilyn and left the shop.

"Some times people like this are caught up in anger because they've been hurt. It's their only way of hiding their real feelings," I said.

"What feelings are those?"

"Deep inside he feels very vulnerable, but if you can get past his anger you will find that spark of God dwelling inside."

"Did you say spark, Jim? Do you mind if I spark up a cigarette?"

"No, and I'm going to get more coffee. Do you want another cup?"

"Maybe I should. Mine has gotten cold," she replied, heading for the door.

In a few minutes she returned. "It sure has gotten cold today. I could only smoke half of a cigarette. I'll be glad when this cold front passes."

"Yes, I'm afraid winter is upon us," I said.

* * *

"Did I tell you about my meditations on John?"

"No, what about John?" She asked as she clicked the tape recorder back on.

"When I want to communicate with him, I put on his baseball hat, get quiet, and allow thoughts of him to come through. From what I can tell he had many interests." Reaching into my wallet I took out a scrap of paper and handed it to her. "Here is just an example of his thirst for knowledge."

She read it and responded. "He says it takes 41.7 days to physically travel one light year at ten times warp speed. I don't understand but I guess it's true."

"I'm not a scientist," I said. "So I can't refute that, but in my meditation I wanted to know about the speed of light. I sent a thought out to ride a beam of light. When I approached the speed of light everything went black. Behind me was light, ahead of me I saw nothing but distant stars. I realized the speed of light was slow compared to other means of travel.

Any question I had about life and the universe John had the answer. He told how a person could find the answer for themselves. He said there was no beginning and no ending of time, but there is a completion of all events. No single big bang, but a series of them, and they will continue happening as long as the universe keeps expanding.

Everything has a cycle and for it to be completed all events have to be experienced. It's the same for an atom as it is for our solar system. Nothing's left undone.

He also said there was only one soul in our solar system, the soul of consciousness in which we all live, and of which we are all a part. Everything is played out in spirit first before it becomes physical. When an idea comes to someone it's already completed in spirit, and when one analyzes it they distort it to fit their experiences. He said that if one writes down an original idea everyone can analyze it whatever way they want.

I've been writing down some of my ideas lately trying to keep them as pure as possible. Sometimes it's only one word, sometimes a sentence. For example, when I asked how life began I got the word 'thought.' That was the symbol. The more I cultivated the word the more diluted it became. I finally settled for. 'A thought created the first strand of consciousness on this lifeless planet.' This was truth for me.

Try it sometime, Marilyn. You'll see what I mean. When you get an insight, notice how pure it is. Write it down before you start analyzing it. Then watch how far you stray from the original truth."

"Yes, I'll try it. Is there anything else that you want to mention in this segment," she asked?

"I have just one thing. John said that eyes are the portholes to the soul. Knowledge is transmitted with the eyes, and so are the seeds of destruction. One must learn to determine what they see in a person's eyes.

When a person is telling the truth you can look into their eyes and see their soul. Their face will radiate truth. It's like looking into the face of babies. You feel the love coming from them.

There is a lot of deceit at this time. It's causing many to rage with anger, but this is a cycle we have to go through to come one step closer to peace. If you know what's happening, you can choose not to be part of it."

"This is a lot to swallow, Jim. Will mankind ever find peace?"

"Yes, but probably not in our lifetime. We are now a *planet of hope* not peace and the energy we are perpetuating will have to run its course. One by one people will become enlightened until eventually enough will tip the scale and dark negative energy will diminish. Until then learn about the different kinds of energy and avoid those that bring you fear, anger, and rage, especially on television. Your life will be easier. When you sense it within, you learn how to change it by thinking of something more pleasant."

"Boy, I wish I could get my hands on his writings. I would like to read them," Marilyn remarked.

"I would too," I said. "They are buried. Charles doesn't want them to fall in the wrong hands. Maybe someday this planet will be ready for them and they'll be published."

Marilyn spoke up. "I've enjoyed today a lot, and I'll be listening to this recording several times. I have to be going. Emily and I are going to do some shopping to jumpstart the holidays."

"Well, have a great day. It's always a pleasure seeing you," I said. On my way home from the coffee shop I was listening to the radio. A plane flying from New York to Europe had exploded in mid air killing everyone on board. I wondered if the passengers knew they had died.

* * *

That evening I got a call from Shirley about a young girl who was in the hospital and who was very ill. Doctors thought she had a cancerous tumor. She wanted to know if Carolyn and I would come and do a healing ceremony on her.

"I feel sympathy for the girl and want to help her, but I'm concerned about the consequences. When do you think we should do it," I asked?

"I'm on the floor until 11 PM. Maybe we could do it after visiting hours are over."

"Shirley, let me call Carolyn to find out if she is free tonight and I will call you back." I didn't want to disappoint Shirley. Having a patient die on her was unacceptable. I was concerned that this might start a trend, one which might gain momentum and I would end up being in the hospital every night healing sick people. Maybe the AMA would find me guilty of practicing medicine without a license.

"I'll wait for your call," she said.

Carolyn wasn't at home. I left a message on her recorder and she called me back later. "I'm not busy tonight and I'd love to participate in healing this girl, but shouldn't we get her parent's permission?

"I'll check with Shirley to see if she'll talk to them," I said. "What time should we meet," she asked?

"How about 9 o'clock at the hospital," I suggested. "Okay. I'll be there," she said and hung up.

I called Shirley telling her what Carolyn said about getting the parent's permission and she said she'd contact them. We arranged to meet at nine.

It was a cold night. We all met in the lobby of the hospital at nine. Shirley led us to the patient's room, and introduced us to the girl's mother who was grateful for any help to heal her daughter. Before we entered Carolyn said. "Is there going to be another person to help us? We really need four people."

Shirley excused herself and was back shortly with another nurse. Then Carolyn said. "Let's make sure our energy is clear. We don't want to contaminate the room with anything but peaceful, loving energy."

The girl was resting with her eyes closed as we entered. Shirley spoke to her. "Your mother is here Brenda."

Her Mother kissed her on the forehead and held her for a moment. Then she said. "These folks are here to help you dear."

We walked to the bed and Shirley spoke. "We are going to have a healing ceremony. It should make you feel more comfortable."

The girl appeared to be about twelve years old, with brown curly hair all messed up from not being combed and sunken cheeks showing signs of the illness. In her eyes I could sense fear, but beyond the fear I sensed a beautiful soul. I felt the energy of love being choked by this illness, and I wanted to assure her everything would be alright.

Carolyn spoke, "Brenda, we are going to perform a healing ceremony. I want to know if that is alright with you. You have a choice. We can't interfere with that, but we want to make you comfortable. I want you to think about the time before you became ill, how healthy and happy you were. Think of a moment when you felt full of life. Now keep thinking of that time while we perform our ceremony. This will not hurt."

I took her feet in my hands. Carolyn held her head, Shirley was on the right side and the other nurse was on the left. We got quiet allowing our minds to scan her body for blockages feeling life force flowing freely around them. Occasionally Brenda let out a sigh when one of us had moved a blockage.

Next we scanned her body with our hands, palms down, not touching it, but seeing energy leave our hands and move through her body. Then Carolyn got her pendulum and began moving it over the body. Every time it found a blockage the pendulum would swing in a big circle. She would inhale and then symbolically blow away the blockage.

After she had successfully completed her survey she said, "All clear.

Let's now send healing energy through her body."

Again we took our positions and felt life force energy entering her forehead and going through her body unhindered by blockages. The whole procedure took about forty minutes.

"I feel so much better now, thanks," Brenda sighed.

Carolyn said to her, "If you want us to come back again we will."

Outside in the hallway, we gathered for a few minutes. I was still concerned that we might be interfering in the girl's evolving process as I didn't know what her issues were in this lifetime. But I was happy to think we did some good. Shirley thanked all of us and said she would let us know how the little girl was progressing. As we were about to leave Brenda's mother came out of the room and thanked us for being there. Carolyn explained to her the meaning behind the ceremony, and if she wanted us to return another time just to let us know. Then, we all departed.

On the way home I was remembering Eric's episode in the hospital and wondered if I would be receiving another visit from angels. After I got home and had a few minutes to relax I asked my higher self about this healing ceremony.

I got that the girl hadn't made a decision whether to stay or leave, and until she did we weren't interfering with spirits watching over her. All we were doing was giving the girl an opportunity to make a decision nothing more.

Once at home, I wanted to know what John would say, I put on his Bronco's hat, sat quietly for a few minutes and waited for his spirit to make its self known. Finally I got a response. "The blockage was residual energy from a previous life. She need not die from it. By cleansing her body you removed the blockages. Children don't have blockages in their body unless they bring them in with them when they are born, or unless they have made an agreement with their parents to address a wrong, or to complete a cycle. A being can finish a life cycle at a very young age and pass on, having no reason to stay around. But for most it takes many years and many lifetimes to complete a cycle. It depends on the magnitude of the cycle and who is involved. That's the way it's supposed to be. That's why you are human," John said.

I thanked him and took off the hat. I wondered what lies ahead. I view my life on an hour by hour, day by day basis. It would take a lot of study and practice to be able to see life from a spirit's viewpoint. I react when my senses are stimulated. I don't wait for my spirit to tell me how to react.

On Wednesday Shirley called me. "The girl's cancerous tumor has shrunk and the doctors are sending her home. It's not a danger to her now, but they are going to keep an eye on it. She feels better and I think we were able to help her in some way."

"We only gave her an opportunity to heal herself," I said. "I'm glad she's better. She's such a sweet girl. Thanks for letting me know. I'll tell Carolyn. Are we still on for this Saturday?"

"Yes, as far as I know. I'm supposed to be off." "Good, I will see you the usual time, bye."

CHAPTER 17

"I forgive myself for ever allowing my power to be diminished by the opinions of others."

On Saturday morning I slept late. When I awoke I had less than an hour to meet Marilyn. I hurried a fast as I could, but had only ten minutes left and it would take me twenty to get there. Carolyn said. "You can stretch time. Just know that you'll be there on time and do not look at your watch. You don't have to drive fast either."

I'll try it. What do I have to lose? Without looking at my watch I backed out of the garage and headed to the coffee shop. I wanted to speed a couple times, but that would destroy the experience. When I pulled up in front of the shop I looked at my watch. I had driven there in ten minutes, but how? I hurried into the shop to tell Marilyn what happened.

"Marilyn," I said excitedly, "Guess what just happened to me. I drove here in ten minutes when it normally takes twenty."

"Oh, there probably isn't much traffic today," she replied. "No, it's really true. I stretched time."

"Stretched time? How do you do that?"

"Just allow yourself to relax, don't look at your watch and see yourself as having plenty of time. It worked. I was really surprised. Carolyn told me to try it sometime and it really works," I said smiling ear to ear.

Marilyn sat with her legs crossed, and got the tape recorder ready for another Saturday morning session. We had become regulars at the coffee shop and people occasionally stopped by our table to ask what we were doing. I suggested that maybe we could meet somewhere else for a change of pace, but the weather had turned colder making the aroma of coffee more enticing. Some of my interview sessions were running rather long but she never complained. In fact she even brought extra tapes just in case.

I set my coffee cup on the table, took a deep breath and began.

* * *

Last summer I realized I was moving further into the metaphysical realm. I didn't know how much longer I would continue going to work at my accounting firm. It no longer satisfied me. I wanted more freedom and more in life than a forty hour work week. But if I quit, I needed something else to do, not only for the money, but also to feed my soul. Would it be possible for me to find a niche in metaphysics to fulfill this dream I'm having? Before I could even think of having a relationship I needed to feel reasonably secure.

I spoke to my inner self and the reply was. "You'll be alright in whatever endeavor you choose. Make your decision and move forward. Allow time to let your future play out on its own without interference."

There was a pause then it continued. "Everyone, human or spirit, has a purpose and a destiny. Allow your destiny to unfold for you. Don't get in the way. Being tired of your job indicates a termination soon, whether by you or by some other means. Your frustration isn't about your job it's your fear of not being accepted in the world you perceive. You feel ridiculed when you publicly mention what you know to be true. You must get over this. Everyone who has ever introduced a new philosophy has been persecuted and you don't want to be in that category. Maybe you should consider working within the boundaries of what is presently accepted to bring about a smooth change. It's acceptable to think and to work towards world peace. Why not create a Center for Intellectual Development and Peace? That would be acceptable and your truths could be slowly interjected without too much difficulty." It felt acceptable and I would think about it.

Later that evening another voice or set of voices came through my mind.

"Don't expose us in your new world." It was the angels again. I hadn't communicated with them since Eric's accident and I didn't want to antagonize them if I could help it. After all they are a part of all that is.

"What do you mean," I inquired?

"We are an anomaly that guard, watch over, and protect man. We have been put on a pedestal by man, given form, and made to look human. We are none of that. If they find out, we could lose their trust, and they will ridicule you, not believe you."

I replied. "Or maybe you will gain from it. Your concern is much like mine. I wouldn't want that to happen to either of us. If we work together it'll elevate both our species." It seemed to satisfy them. Whenever there is discord a solution can always be found.

Whenever I have had a confrontation with anyone, if I go to a safe place where both of us are on equal ground, a solution can be found that is acceptable to all. I relaxed further and fell asleep in the chair. When I awoke it was the middle of the night, I couldn't remember anything I had meditated on and went to bed.

The next morning as I sat on the side of the bed my meditation came back to me, as though all my thoughts had completed themselves. A voice from inside said to me. "The desire for your knowledge to be accepted is admirable, but you aren't the first person to want to do this. It's an ongoing process. Scientists are constantly striving to prove their theories. What you want people to know, is that other forms of intelligence exist, and people are communicating with them whether they realize it or not."

I thought of work and lost the connection. I don't want to be late again. I had been late too many times recently. Maybe the voice was right. Was I seeking a way of getting fired? I'll have to show more enthusiasm for my job.

A few days later I had a dentist appointment. I needed a crown put on a tooth and chose a dentist who ran a very efficient office. I also thought he was a gentle man.

The first thing the dentist did was touch me on the shoulder which relaxed me, and made me feel he appreciated my being there. I thought more professionals should become personal with their clients. He was cheerful and we talked a few minutes. I said. "You really like what you are doing, don't you."

The dentist replied, "Yes, I do. It makes me happy. When I stop enjoying my work I'll quit. I have other challenges I still want to do with my life. This is my third profession. First I was a teacher. I enjoyed it while I was teaching, but when I started getting bored I changed to psychiatry. After that I became a dentist. I've been doing this for many years, and I still enjoy it as much as the day I started."

With my mouth full of dental equipment I couldn't ask any more questions but I got to thinking. I'm really tired of doing taxes for others year after year, and spending those long hours at tax time. There are other things I would like to accomplish before I leave this planet. Maybe it is time to move on. I could tell by my feelings I was only there for my paycheck, but I had become bored.

I didn't take my decision too lightly. I had butterflies in my stomach when I handed in my resignation the next day. My boss suggested I take a few months off and help out in the spring at tax time when they could use the help. It made good sense to me. I wondered why I hadn't thought of it, but I would be without a paycheck until spring. That scared me, but at least my boss kept the door open and I could always go back to work if I needed to. I had a retirement plan but it didn't kick in until my actual retirement. I was only fifty-four, far too soon to be retired.

I drove north to Seattle for two weeks. It was the first vacation I had since Doris became ill. When I got back to Denver I was anxious to do something. I set about fixing up my house. When that was accomplished I started getting bored. I still had my meditation class.

One night Carolyn suggested I should teach a class in metaphysics at the free university. It got me to thinking. With my knowledge I could surely put together a class that would draw students, so for the next few weeks I started organizing materials to teach. Ouizi, being a teacher, volunteered to help me put the class together.

There were two classes I wanted to teach, one, getting to know your psychic self, the other on psychic thought. I went to the university with my proposal, but it was too late for that season. They could offer it in the spring, and I told them I would let them know.

* * *

Just then, the angry young man from last week came up to our table. Marilyn stopped the recorder as he began speaking. "I thought about what you said last week. I almost had an accident, and could have used the extra caffeine in my system. I tend to be an angry person and I don't mean to be. Most people avoid me, but you didn't. Thanks."

"I knew you to be a kind person. I could see it deep inside you. You just have to learn how to handle your anger and the real you will shine thru."

Marilyn excused herself to go for a cigarette. The not so angry man and I spoke a few more minutes before he walked over to get his coffee. This time the clerk gave him a big smile. His energy was totally different. What a change.

"Is there anything else we need to go over this week before we break up today?" Marilyn asked before sitting down.

"No, I'm finished. Will I see you next Saturday," I asked? "I plan to be here."

"Okay. Have a good week," she responded. "Yes, you have one too, bye."

CHAPTER 18

*"Heaven and earth rejoice each time a human
realizes and accepts his divinity."*

The following Saturday Marilyn looked different, dressed in a sweater and slacks instead of her usual blouse and short skirt. She acknowledged my entrance while scanning through a book on self-publishing.

"I can't find a publisher for your book and want to explore the option of self-publishing it," she said. "Working with you on your biography has given me a lot of incite, and it has caused me to get more involved in the process."

"I'm glad I've been able to contribute something. It's been good for me because it has given me an opportunity to ponder my life. It makes me feel that my life is worthwhile. Did I tell you about my confrontation with a bear last summer?"

"No," she commented clicking on her tape recorder.

* * *

Eric and I went camping last August two weeks before I met you. He had replaced the telescope and camera destroyed in the accident. The doctors had removed the plaster cast on his arm the week before and he wanted to try out his new equipment before he started teaching. He was hoping to get some good pictures to use when he started teaching astronomy.

We have a favorite campsite, and from past experience we decided to go early as the individual campsites along the stream filled quickly on weekends. If the sites were taken we would have to stay in the camping area maintained by the Forest Service.

We found our favorite spot vacant and established camp along the river. Then we went scouting for a good place to set up Eric's equipment. We needed a site away from any lights so stars would shine their brightest and a clearing so trees would not interfere. We ventured up the mountain side to an area above the campground with only one gnarled tree to work around. We made sure our path wouldn't be too difficult to follow at night and went back to the camp ground.

When we returned a couple with a motor home next to our campsite welcomed us. They had been camping there all week and had been speaking to a Forest Service ranger. He said bears had been raiding trash cans in the area and not to put any food in the cans. They suggested that we keep all food in the car for safety, and not in our tent.

We thanked them for their suggestions and decided to gather scrap wood for our campfire after putting away the food. Pickings were meager and we were happy we had purchased two bundles of wood before leaving the city. Several fishermen were trying their luck in the stream flowing placidly by our camp. It felt so peaceful watching fishermen fly casting on the stream. Why would anyone want to leave such a serene place?

In the evening Eric started a small fire while I prepared hamburgers and beans on the camp stove. Then we sat around the campfire until it was totally dark. I was concerned about bears roaming the area, but Eric didn't think we would have any problems. "There are too many people in the area for them to cause much trouble," he said.

We had brought two powerful flashlights with us so that we could find our way in the dark. Eric packed his equipment on his back, I carried water and camera gear, and we headed up the path towards our chosen site. It took us about twenty minutes and we were happy that the lights from the campground and the city didn't interfere with our gazing.

Eric set up his equipment attaching the camera to the telescope and began watching the movement of the stars. As he found various formations he pointed them out to me and took a picture of them. I tried to show enthusiasm to give him encouragement, but stargazing was not my real purpose for being here. It was just an excuse for spending time with my son, and getting away from the city for a few days. I did want to do some meditating in a peaceful setting.

My son wasn't a social person. It was hard to discover where his interests lay socially. I always felt he needed an anchor and maybe his interest in the stars was his anchor.

"Eric, are you dating anyone," I asked? "You never bring anyone home. Are you content with just stars and computers? Isn't there something else that interests you, like girls?"

"You are one to talk," he fired back. You've hardly shown any interest in women since Mom died until recently with Shirley."

I didn't realize I touched a nerve. "It took me a long time to get over your Mom," I said. "When you love someone as much as I loved your Mother you don't soon get over it. I guess you are like me. My interest in metaphysics occupies much of my time. Your interest in astronomy occupies yours. I didn't mean to pry."

"I have an occasional date, Dad, but I don't want to encourage something that's not there. It's not that I haven't tried. I'm waiting for someone like Mom to come along. I want to have the love relationship you had with her. I'm not willing to settle for less. Besides I have Grandma, you and a few buddies at school. I'm not lonely, but I do hope the right person comes along before I get too old."

"I don't think you will have to worry about that, son. You have a lot to offer. Take your time. You'll know when the time is right."

We sat watching stars for maybe two hours when we heard some twigs snap. Someone or something was approaching. We hadn't turned on our flashlights as we had wanted total darkness. Unless they heard us talking no one would know we were there. The sounds came closer. It was coming in our direction on the path we had taken. I felt my back stiffen not quite knowing what to do. "Maybe if we remain quiet it will go away," I whispered.

"Sh-h-h," Eric motioned.

All of a sudden a big black bear appeared. Acting as one we flashed our lights on it. The bear was as startled as we were. He rose on his hind legs as if to pounce as we scrambled to our feet. There he was, fangs showing, paws ready to strike, the biggest bear I'd ever seen, and only a few feet away. One swipe of those paws and it would all be over. Both lights on his face probably blinded him. Neither of us knew what to do next. For a moment we froze, suspended in time. Afraid to breathe my heart was in my stomach. Eric was breathing heavily and ready to panic.

Then the bear turned around and was gone as quickly as he had come, but it seemed forever. We stood there trying to catch our breath. Finally Eric spoke. "That was a close call. I'm never going to come up here alone."

"I know what you mean. Me neither. I guess we should have stayed closer to our campsite." We hastily put the equipment back in their cases and cautiously made our way down the hillside fearing we might bump into the bear again waiting for its next meal.

Once back at camp we felt safer. We rekindled the campfire as neither of us was ready to turn in. Watching the fire we were deep in thought. I was playing the—*what if*—game. What if he had killed Eric or me? I didn't save him to be eaten by a bear. What if he comes into our camp while we are sleeping? I wouldn't have time to summon spiritual help. It is one thing to know what you are up against, another to have just a split second to act. I was just happy the bear didn't attack.

I tossed and turned all night. Eric was also having a difficult time sleeping. What if the bear would enter our campsite or break into our car for the food? I had to get a hold of myself. If the bear was going to harm us he would have done so, but my negative side said, "Maybe he's saving you for a snack later." It's amazing how the mind wonders. This was a test of my mental abilities, of my will power. In a split second it can change from a positive reality to a negative one. Tonight I was playing both realities at once. No wonder I couldn't sleep.

In the morning we were both awake at dawn. We discussed whether to stay the rest of the weekend or go back to town. We decided to stay as the night went without trouble in the campsite near other people.

The sun was shining and the day would be warm. The aroma of brewing coffee permeated the area. After we finished breakfast Eric excused himself saying he wanted to take a hike, but I was more interested in having a good meditation on a rock somewhere in the sun. I wasn't quite ready to leave the safety of the campsite.

A big rock by the stream had caught my attention and I decided it would be just right. I sat on it facing the sun and quieted my thoughts. It was so peaceful, the sound of the water running over pebbles, birds singing, and the scent of fresh pine in my nose. I tried to clear my mind, but still held mental energy on last night's encounter. "Do we all panic when faced with survival? Why can't we just acknowledge that these events exist and go on with our life peacefully?" I'm sure the bear didn't intend to kill us. It was as scared as we were, yet its sheer size made its demise less likely. But nothing happens without a reason. What was the reason for last night's event? As I continued my analysis my fear subsided and peace finally came. I meditated for a long time.

When I opened my eyes I saw a wild cat silently observing me from the edge of the campsite. My panic bell rang again, but this time I was in control. I wasn't going to let it get the better of me. Calmly I watched as the cat approached my rock then leaped effortlessly to one nearby. It cleared a six foot hurdle without a pause. For only a second it stood there in its magnificence. His head held high, king of the forest, he scanned the surroundings before descending the other side, disappearing into the forest. I didn't know whether to be excited or scared, but it definitely ended my meditation.

When Eric returned I told him about my encounter, but somehow it didn't seem to arouse his feelings. Having forgotten the bear incident the night before, Eric had been scouting out a place closer to the camp for his star gazing for later that night. Maybe living through the accident had made him fearless about surviving, and then maybe kids just take life for granted.

That night we observed the stars again. Although light from campfires in the valley interfered, Eric still got some great pictures which he saved for his astronomy class.

Sunday we packed up and came back to town. Eric got the pictures he wanted and I got to spend time with him.

* * *

"I liked the bear story. How often does anyone come face to face with a bear in the wild? Most people I know have never even seen one in the mountains," Marilyn remarked. "I need a cigarette. Do you mind?"

We put on our coats and went outside so she could light up. "You know, someday I'm going to stop smoking. I don't find them as exciting anymore. I guess I'm outgrowing my need."

"Marilyn, I smoked in college and got hooked. It took a lot of will power to break the habit. Today they have patches you can put on to help, but they didn't have them when I quit. I had to do it cold turkey. You might try the patches."

"I just need to find a good reason," she said.

"If you saw what my wife went through it would give you a good reason," I said before remembering that it didn't stop Edward's smoking. "Did I tell you about my meditation last week?"

"No," she responded.

"Do you remember the airplane that crashed recently? It exploded in mid air."

"Yes, everyone was killed. It was terrible."

"I asked my guides where the spirits were of those who died, and was surprised when I was told they were still in the airplane unaware an explosion had occurred. Until they were aware that the accident happened and that they had died, they would be suspended in time.

In the meditation I took myself to the location of the craft as though I was a passenger, and began a conversation with those on board. When I told them about the accident and said they were dead they laughed at me. I asked them to think of their loved ones and the sorrow they were feeling. Then they began to disappear. With only a few left I put my hand through the fuselage of the plane and suggested they could do the same. When they did they became scared. I convinced them to go with me into the light where others were waiting for them."

Marilyn interrupted me. "You mean that sometimes people die and aren't aware they've passed on?"

"Yes, they haven't gone through the dying process and are left in a kind of limbo. Until they are informed they continue flying in the plane, driving their car or living through explosions. Anytime an accident occurs where someone dies someone should check to see if the spirit of the victim is suspended at the scene.

That's why the dying process is so important. It separates the spirit from the body so it can move on.

I'll never forget the pain I felt losing Doris. That's why I'm trying to learn about the spirit world. It seems to me the only distinctive permanent part of us is our spirit. Do you understand?"

"Yes, I do, Jim. I fear my Mother getting sick and dying. It's something I don't want to face right now. I just don't know what I'll do when that time comes."

"If you try to understand the spirit of your Mother, her beliefs, how she does things, like the way she treats you, and her contribution to humanity, then it'll be easier for you to let go when she does decide to pass.

We all make agreements with each other. You have them with your Mother and with your friends. Some you made in past lives that you will complete in this life. You even have one with me that goes beyond writing my biography, which concerns your own personal enlightenment. It's no surprise you became a writer. There's a purpose behind every career. Your career helps you to learn what you most want to know. Writing is an excellent way to organize and put on paper what you know to be your truth."

"I haven't thought of life that way. I sure have a lot to learn."

"Not only do you put it on paper but you script it in a way as to make people want to read it, but the real benefactor is you, the creator of the work.

Like any work of art one takes pride in their accomplishment."

"We've discussed my need to write but what are you trying to learn in this life. What made you want to learn about the spirit," she asked?

"It's a long story, but if you have time today I will be glad to oblige." "Yes. Let's have another cup of coffee and I'll put a new tape in the recorder."

CHAPTER 19

"Everything that happens is worked out in spirit before it becomes physical."

I sat across from Marilyn explaining my philosophy. "Aging was my catalyst for learning about spirit." She sat there intently listening and trying to take in every word. Her desire to write and the attention she had been paying me added enthusiasm to my thoughts. It seemed the more I told her about spirit the more excited she got.

"I knew there had to be more to life than just keeping my body fit, and physical exercise was occupying much of my time. When Doris got sick I literally forgot about exercise, and took care of her. After she died I pursued spiritual knowledge. My brain exploded with exciting new ways of looking at life and at the universe.

I learned to meditate on a particular spirit drawing its energy to me. I meditated on the spirit of Jesus asking what I needed to do to ascend. He said I hadn't developed the energy or discipline necessary to accomplish such a feat, but I could learn. It scares me too much to pursue it. I love living too much, but now that my body is starting to wear out I'm having doubts. Ascension is still a possibility but I don't know anyone else who has done so except possibly John.

Marilyn, I feel positive about life until something happens to challenge my beliefs. When someone dear to me criticizes me, it zaps my power. It happened at my house on Thanksgiving a few weeks ago."

* * *

Mom cooked the Thanksgiving turkey. Edward, Ellen, their daughter Stacy, and Eric were at my house. Figurines were put out of reach and things that would intrigue a child out of sight. The women were in the kitchen putting finishing touches on the feast, I was on the floor playing with my three year old Granddaughter. The boys were watching television.

Something caught my attention on television and for a few seconds I forgot about Stacy. When I turned back she was gone and nowhere to be found.

Edward jumped me, shouting at me for not watching her. We have had disagreements but he never raised his voice to me like that before. I took it personally. We exchanged a few hot words bringing the women from the kitchen to see what the ruckus was.

Ellen looked in the back yard. Eric took to the basement, and Mom checked all the rooms. Edward and I grabbed our coats and headed outdoors, each going a different direction.

I had to control myself and to forget the confrontation. I tabled my anger for later. It was too stressful and I needed to focus my energy on finding Stacy. I cleared my mind and with only one request for my higher self. 'Lead me to Stacy.'

Walking slowly, I paused waiting to feel her energy, then walked in the direction spirit led me. Two blocks away I found her talking to a neighbor. It was quite a ways for a child to travel so quickly. The adult was concerned that a small child was out by herself without a coat, and wasn't even crying. Stacy didn't show any fear and must have had a strong spirit guiding her.

Thanking the neighbor, I put my coat around her and carried her back to the house. They were all still accusing each other of not watching her but quieted down as we entered.

Ellen rushed to us noticing how cold Stacy was and decided to give her a bath to warm her up. With Stacy's asthmatic condition she didn't want a chill to cause a reaction. As she removed Stacy's dress I noticed a birthmark on her back I hadn't seen before. It was in the same area as Doris' birthmark had been.

"When are you two going to act like grownups and get over your differences?" Mom spoke in a stern voice pointing to Edward and me. I don't know why you two can't act more like Father and son. Why do you have to be so cold to each other? Every time we get together you give each other the cold shoulder. Can't we have just one Thanksgiving in peace?"

I hadn't seen Mom so upset before. We didn't need this discord. Having Stacy disappear was stressful enough.

To Edward I said. "I apologize for not watching Stacy more closely." "That's okay, Dad. I shouldn't have mouthed off like that. It's just that when I was a kid, my real Dad disappeared on me and I never got over that feeling of loss. When Stacy couldn't be found that fear came back."

I had no idea that Edward's feelings were so deep. He managed to cover them up so completely. It made me feel closer to him than I had felt in years.

"Glad that's settled," Mom said. "It's nobody's fault. Children do these things. Let's not let it destroy the day. We are supposed to be thankful. Come on, sit down to dinner and let's give thanks."

Stacy was back in the room all cheery-eyed ready to see what other mischief she could get into.

* * *

"Marilyn, I wanted to tell them how I found her, but knew that Edward wouldn't understand. I didn't want to rile him further.

"What's the problem between you and Edward?" She spoke, gulping a slug of cold coffee? "You two haven't gotten along since he was young. What happened to create this tension?"

"I don't know," I said rubbing my brow. "Wish I did. He's resentful about something from his childhood and won't let it go. Until he's ready, I'll just have to wait. When Doris and I met we made an agreement in spirit as well as physically to take care of each other, and part of the agreement was for me to be a Father to her son. I thought I had, but somewhere I messed up.

I hope it's not too late to heal wounds."

"Speaking of late, I have to go home," she said, looking at her watch and shutting off her recorder. Mom and I are going Christmas shopping this afternoon. I hope the stores aren't too crowded."

"Are we still on for next Saturday," I asked?

"Yes same time same place, same station," she said laughing.

"I'd like to take you to lunch next week. Can you spend some extra time with me, sort of a Christmas celebration?"

"I'd enjoy that. I won't schedule anything else. See you next Saturday."

I knew we were nearing the end of our Saturday escapades, and I felt like celebrating. After all it was the holiday season.

On my way home I was thinking about Stacy's birthmark. Why should she have one and why would it be in the same place as Doris'. I hadn't noticed it before. I called Charles when I got home to see if he had an answer to my question.

"Hello, Charles. It's Jim."

Betty answered the phone. "No, Charles is out jogging with our oldest son. He should be home shortly. Can I have him call you when he comes in?"

"Yes, have him give me a ring. Thanks." A short time later he returned my call.

"Jim, this is Charles. How are you?"

"I'm fine, but I have a question for you. Did your Uncle John write about reincarnation?"

"I don't recall. There probably were a few papers on the subject. Why do you ask?"

"My Granddaughter has a birthmark on her back and I wonder if it's a carry-over from a past life? Do you suppose that Stacy is Doris reincarnated?"

"I recall reading that a person carries birthmarks and disabilities through many lifetimes until the energy causing them is withdrawn. When energy is created it expands as long as it's fed. After that it collapses on itself. Is there anything else that might indicate they are one in the same?"

"Oh, yes. She has a mild case of asthma." "Did Doris have asthma?"

"No, but she did cough a lot before she died. Do you suppose her coughing had anything to do with the asthma," I asked?

Charles replied. "There's a fine line between life and death. The heart and chest area are heavily involved with emotions. Whatever caused Doris to smoke, eventually getting cancer is energy that could be carried over to Stacy in the form of asthma. If Stacy doesn't create an issue to strengthen it, the asthma may diminish over time."

I asked. "Will you be at the meeting next Thursday? Maybe we could discuss it further then."

"Yes, let's talk about it then," Charles replied.

* * *

At the meditation I brought up the subject of reincarnation to the group. Everyone except Sara believed in it. Sara believed that when a North American Indian died its spirit remained with the living, and did not return into form.

Carolyn suggested. "When a person dies they take their newly acquired wisdom with them as well as issues not resolved in that lifetime. During one's lifetime issues are completed and new ones are created. Unresolved issues are taken with them into their next life, and are worked out by agreement with the individuals who helped to create them. Doris had a chest problem and so does Stacy."

It made good sense to me, but Charles surprised us when he took a piece of paper out of his wallet, one that had been written on by John. "I couldn't find anything new about reincarnation in my Uncles writings, but I found this writing which I thought might be appropriate. It read,

"Information from the spirit, Jethro, was written upon my return from a trip to the planet Dos.

'What a special gift these physical bodies are to us spirits. Without them we would roam the galaxy, unanchored, creating whatever we want but unable to fully experience our creations. The added dimensions these bodies give, allows us to see, smell and touch our creation. Without the experience we have nothing to give back to mass consciousness."

"It sounds to me that spirits need physical bodies in order to experience life and they make agreements with other spirits to aid them in the completion of those experiences," I suggested.

Carolyn piped up. "It means that consciousness expands through each person's experience and the agreements we make often take lifetimes to complete. If there were ways to track spirits as they go from one life to another we could get a better idea of how it works."

Ouizi's face lit up. "I have an idea," she suggested. "Instead of just drawing a family tree one could include a profile of each person with information on their personality, talents, looks, scars, and ailments. That way when they surface again it would indicate who is possibly returning."

"Great idea, Ouizi, I wouldn't have to go back very far to link Doris to my Granddaughter, Stacy."

"Eyes are a giveaway," Sara remarked. I get a lot of information about a person's character from their eyes."

Our meditation was short that evening as it had snowed and we were concerned about driving home. We thanked Charles for sharing John's writings and left.

On the way home I was thinking that Doris and Edward worked well together and were very close. If they had been husband and wife in another time it wouldn't have surprised me. Eric, Mom and I are close, and we are the same way. Each of us knows what the others are thinking before they speak.

If I died, I would like to come back as Eric's son. I wondered if gender made a difference. If a male always comes back as a male, but how would one explain effeminate men? I knew there was not a gender in spirit, but there probably were energies that accentuate ruggedness and gentility.

The topic of reincarnation weighed heavily on my mind keeping me awake. I restlessly tossed back and forth thinking of all the possibilities. Unless John had the answers, no one else I knew ever tried to learn about spirits. I wondered if I would ever get to read all of his writings. Maybe someday Charles would let me borrow them.

I was glad Marilyn was putting into print what I had learned about spirit over the last few years. I wanted others to read what I had learned about the hereafter and to understand how they can influence what happens to them. The universe is so vast. Information that lies in consciousness is far greater than all the libraries and computers on the planet. For every profession there are vast areas of knowledge waiting to be tapped.

What I needed now was to shut off my mind so I could get some sleep.

CHAPTER 20

Integrity means you will not sacrifice the principles by which you live.

It was Saturday morning and right on schedule she was waiting for me. I have a surprise in store for Marilyn this morning and could hardly keep it secret. "Good morning," I said full of excitement. "What a great day!"

"Good morning Jim," she answered noticing my unusually good mood. "I've been organizing my notes, and I think I have enough information to get started laying out the chapters of your book. Are we still going to have lunch today?"

"Yes, and I have a surprise for you, someone I want you to meet." I walked up to the counter and ordered two house coffees, handing one to Marilyn who already had an empty cup. "Why are you so upbeat today," she asked?

"I awoke this morning from a festive dream in full color. I was floating down from an upper story, on the outside of a building. There were lots of people milling around on the grass below. Everything was vivid and I felt great. When I showered a spirit guide give me information about consciousness. Would you like to hear what this guide told me?"

"Yes," she said turning on her tape recorder.

"You know, everyone has guides and can communicate with them if they have the patience and desire to learn how.

I was filled with wonder about what my guide had to say. He said that consciousness is like one trillion radio stations all on different frequencies. A person can tune into anyone of them. What keeps them from hearing two stations at once is the brain which generally has only one channel open at a time. Every living thing is a station giving and receiving vibrations. Sometimes you tune into a station that is energetic and full of life. Other times you tune into one that is sad and depressive. Each person has their own vibration signature which enables them to communicate with similar vibrations of others. If you turn your signal to a frequency of fear you attract fearful things.

Can you imagine all this information going on at once and people having a difficult time determining what they want to listen to? We take our bodies for granted. We use them, abuse them, and eventually wear them out. Our bodies take a lot of punishment and seem to survive despite all the torture we inflict on them. Have you ever thought how much knowledge had to be accumulated in order to create a human being? We haven't and maybe never will have a computer capable of handling all that information. Still, it's out there floating around in our atmosphere just waiting for someone to tap into it.

We can create new life from our bodies. How is that possible? Who discovered how to put a body together that can recreate? The information isn't written down, but it's available in consciousness. You are probably going to say, 'It's God,' but I think we all have a hand in it. Every thought we have, everything we create, every experience goes back to God. I don't think God had all this information when the planet gave its first breath. I think God evolves through our experiences. Consciousness absorbs every thought, be it from plant, animal, or man."

"That's mind boggling," she said. "I can't fathom the vastness of what you just said. I do know that if we can learn to harness the energy and vibrations you are talking about there will be no limits to our capabilities."

Just as she was sipping her coffee a tall dark haired young man walked up to our table. "Good morning Dad. May I join you," he asked?

"Good morning Eric," I replied. "You got here just on time. The conversation was a bit intense. I needed to lighten up. Marilyn, I want you to meet my son Eric." Turning to his son, Jim said. "This is the writer I've been telling you about."

"Pleased to meet you," Eric said. "I know how intense Dad's conversation can get at times. I hope he's not boring you."

"No, I'm fascinated by his stories. I have recorded most of them," she said turning off her recorder. "Your Dad tells me you are teaching Astronomy at the university this year. How's it going?"

"I love it." Eric exclaimed full of excitement. "I didn't realize how difficult it is to teach a group of students, and I've been expanding my lesson plan to keep up with them. I'm sure I'll get the hang of it by the end of the semester. They also want me to teach an advanced course which I'm looking forward to doing next semester. That'll give me two classes which will sure help pay my bills."

"Was it hard making the adjustment from student to teacher," she asked? "No, but I didn't realize how young college freshmen appear, and I'm only a few years older than they are. Was I really that naive? Probably," Eric answered his own question.

"After I graduated I noticed the same thing," she responded. "Would any one like a cup of coffee," I asked?

"Not for me, but I would like a cigarette." Turning to Eric she said. "Would you go outside with me so I can have a smoke?"

"Sure," he responded quickly and followed her out the door.

This left me standing alone. 'Well, I may as well get another cup for myself,' I thought, turning towards the counter. I think I'll splurge and have a latte.

One cigarette became two, and a half hour later they were still conversing. I could tell they were enjoying each other's company. Was I getting jealous or just becoming impatient? No, I'll let them have their fun. They didn't even notice when Mom and Shirley walked past them.

"Good morning," Shirley said cheerily as they entered the coffee shop. They came to the table and I stood to receive a big hug from both of them.

"I'm glad we could meet for lunch, but I have to be at work at three this afternoon. Where is this young woman I'm supposed to be jealous of," Shirley asked?

"She's outside talking to Eric," I countered.

Mom said, "I noticed them when we came in. She's very pretty. Maybe he'll ask her for a date. He needs a girl in his life, you know."

"My Mother, the match maker," I grinned, winking at her. "She's a fine human being. I'd totally approve."

We spoke for a while waiting for the other two to come back inside. Finally I went outside to get them. "I have some people for you to meet inside Marilyn. Would you join us," I asked? We walked back inside and I said to Marilyn. "I want you to meet my Mother and Shirley." They shook hands and sat down.

"It's a pleasure to meet your whole family. Now I'm finally able to put a face to a name. It helps to give me a better perspective on your life, Jim."

"Dad, I thought you said we were going to have lunch," Eric said.

I replied. "Yes, I am getting hungry. Marilyn, will you join us for lunch?" "I'd love to have lunch with all of you. We can really get acquainted."

"I've made reservations at the restaurant down the street. We can walk to it," I suggested. "Mom, do you feel up to it?"

"If we take it slow, I'll be fine," she answered.

The air was nippy, but the warmth of the sun made for a beautiful day. We casually walked towards the restaurant, Mom, Shirley, and I leading, while Marilyn and Eric trailed behind.

"We have reservations in the name of Roberts," I said to the receptionist as we entered.

"Right this way please," the hostess answered taking us to a table by the window.

Shirley and Mom sat on one side, the two kids on the other, and I sat on the end facing the window.

The orders were taken and we sat there chatting until the food arrived. Marilyn had lots of questions for everyone. The two kids looked so good sitting next to each other that Mom remarked about it several times making them both blush. After the dishes were cleared away conversation finally slowed. I noticed Mom was making faces as though uncomfortable. "Mom, are you alright," I asked?

"I think it's just a little indigestion," she answered. "I'll be fine in a few minutes."

Shirley looked at her and in a tone that only a seasoned nurse could express, she asked. "When was the last time you saw a doctor about your heart?"

"Six months ago right after my operation."

"That was a year ago, Mom. Haven't you seen him since," I asked?

"I don't remember," she replied.

"Maybe it would be a good idea to set up another appointment." Shirley said.

"But my by-pass should last a while. Do you really think I need to be examined?" Mom was being assertive.

"It's better to be safe than sorry. Then you will know for sure you only had indigestion and not something more serious."

"Christmas is only a few days away. I'll call my doctor for an examination after the holidays."

I interrupted, "Are you sure you should wait that long?"

"I don't want anything to interfere with the Christmas Eve party at my condo." Looking at Marilyn she said. "You are invited also if you want to come."

"I'd be delighted to come," Marilyn replied.

Just like Mother, changing the subject. She didn't like anyone making a fuss over her. Once she made up her mind that was it. "Okay Mom, but right after the holidays I want you to see the doctor. Promise me you will?"

"Yes, Son, right after the holidays."

Shirley talked to Mom quietly for a few minutes making suggestions on how to handle her chest pains reminding her to take it easy. She offered to help her prepare the food for the party and Mom quickly accepted her offer. The kids were talking about upcoming events when I heard Marilyn ask Eric if he would like to go with her to the Club that evening. I was glad that Eric was taking an interest in her.

We all walked back to the coffee shop and departed. Marilyn had come by bus and Eric was quick to offer her a ride home which she accepted.

I thanked Shirley for bringing my Mom and I took her home.

Mom was resting when I called her later in the day. As the conversation ended I asked her about the doctor. "Will you promise me to see him soon?"

"Yes Son, I'll call for an appointment first thing Monday morning. "Do you want me to take you to church tomorrow," I asked?

"No, I'm going on the bus with the other seniors."

"Well, I guess I'll see you at your place on Christmas Eve then."

"OK, talk to you later, Jim. I had a wonderful day. Thanks for inviting me."

"You are welcome. Please take care of yourself. I don't want to lose you.

Bye Mom."

"Bye son."

CHAPTER 21

Everyone should write a book.
The workings of each inner mind are important to humanity.

On Christmas Eve, Shirley and I arrived early to help with the cooking. Mom had a small artificial tree on the table by the window with lights and old fashioned ornaments. She was in the kitchen making her famous mashed potatoes when we arrived. I saw her adding lots of butter and inquired why she was still using so much. "The doctor told you to watch your cholesterol, Mom," I said.

"This is a holiday and I'll use as much butter as I want," she replied.

I suggested she use margarine, but she wanted that buttery taste, and that was the end of the conversation.

The doorbell rang and I went to greet Edward, Ellen and their daughter Stacy. Ellen went to the kitchen to see if she could help out, and Stacy followed her. Edward and I sat in the living room and talked football. The doorbell rang again and Eric and Marilyn came in. Eric joined us in the living room while Marilyn checked out the action in the kitchen.

Shortly, we sat down to a wonderful meal, stuffing ourselves and enjoying the conversation. When dinner was over Marilyn and Eric went out on the balcony so that she could smoke, and we sat around the table chatting. Stacy found a coloring book with crayons and was busy creating a masterpiece of color.

We then gathered in the living room and passed around gifts. I brought an enlarged picture of my Dad which I had framed for Mom. It was a copy of the one she had on her night stand.

Mom had wrapped a box containing the old hand carved locomotive I'd been given on my first Christmas, the one I forgot to bring with me when we moved out west years ago. It had been carved by grandpa, and she found it stored in the attic of her Mom's house after grandma's funeral.

Edward and his family left right after the gifts were passed out, and we sat there conversing when Shirley spoke out. "Mrs. Roberts, I smell smoke. Did we leave a burner on in the kitchen?"

"I don't think so," she replied.

I rushed into the kitchen to check it out. Nothing was left on, but I smelled smoke, too.

"It must be coming from another unit," Eric chimed in. He went to the front door and opened it. Smoke was starting to cloud the hallway. I noticed that smoke was coming from under the unit door at the end of the hall.

"Mom, whose unit is at the end of the hall," I asked? "That's Sarah James' unit," she answered.

"Call the office," I said, as I rushed down the hall and tried the door. It wouldn't budge. It wasn't hot but the smoke was getting thicker and was beginning to burn my eyes. God, please help me open this door. I pushed against the door and all of a sudden it opened. I took a deep breath and went into the room. Barely able to see my way around I put a handkerchief over my nose and mouth feeling my way towards the bedroom. There I tripped over something hitting my head on the bedpost. It took a moment to regain my equilibrium and I knelt down to see what it was. Sarah had passed out on the floor.

I pulled a blanket off the bed, wrapped it around her, gathered her in my arms and headed back out the front door. Once in the hall I carried her to Mom's unit and put her on the sofa. Shirley immediately started administering CPR to her. Only then did I realize the gravity of what I had done. I felt faint, my legs went limp, and I had to sit down. Everyone was staring wide-eyed at me as though they couldn't believe I'd been so courageous in what I had just done.

Eric was the first one to say anything. Stuttering he exclaimed, "Dad, you—you walked through the door." "What did you say," I asked?

"You walked through the door," he said slowly weighing every word.

"You've got to be kidding. I opened the door and walked in. Then, I brought her out through the door."

"No," Marilyn said. You walked through the door. It never opened." "That's not true. Nobody can walk through a door." Tracing my movements I said. "I got up from my chair, walked down the hall, and turned the handle. It was locked. I tried it again, and it still wouldn't open. Then I leaned against it, and it—" stopping in mid-sentence. I couldn't remember what happened except it opened.

"How do you explain that," Eric remarked?

"I must have locked it when I came out," but I knew that wasn't so. I don't know what happened, but thank you God for being there.

Just then the elevator door opened and the firemen came down the hall, the night watchman rushing ahead of them. He fumbled for the keys and unlocked the deadbolt. Putting on their masks the fireman rushed into the unit. In a moment they were back out. Sarah had forgotten to turn off the burner on the kitchen stove. A pot had boiled dry and was smoking the grease in the tray under the burner. Then the paramedics arrived, and were shown to Mom's condo where they administered to Sarah, deciding to take her to the emergency room.

By this time other residents were in the hallway wanting to know what was going on. One of them mentioned that the woman was becoming senile and would probably need to go to assisted care, 'poor soul'. I wondered how many more years it would be before Mom would be in the same predicament, but that's what retirement communities were all about, to take care of you to the end. I was thankful that Mom had so many friends.

As quickly as it happened, it quieted down, almost as though it was an everyday occurrence. I asked Mom, "Does this happen often? Everyone seems so calm."

"No, but it does happen and we get used to it. None of us here are getting any younger. It's nice to know we have each unit set up for emergencies. You never know when someone's going to fall and need help. Each unit is wired into the main switchboard and into emergency. It gives us peace of mind so there's no real need to call 911."

Thinking of Mom's heart problem I asked. "By the way, have you made your appointment with the Doctor?"

"Yes, I've taken care of it." That was all she said and changed the subject. "Eric said you walked through Sarah's door. Is this something new you are learning in your meditation class?"

"No Mother, I can't explain it. It must have been a miracle."

Eric was listening and exclaimed. "My Dad, the hero, I'm proud of you."

The conversation continued, but I was deep in thought. Did I actually walk through a solid object? I knew that spirit could do amazing things, but I'd never thought that I could accomplish such a feat. The experience left me exhausted and I still had to take Shirley home before I could relax.

"I think it's time to leave," I remarked.

"Yes," Shirley said, I still need to wrap some presents for my niece. I'm spending Christmas with my sister's daughter tomorrow."

Eric and Marilyn said their good-byes and she said. "Wow, Jim, this will make a terrific ending for your book.

"It's just one of those everyday miracles," I replied, trying to shrug it off.

We got in the elevator and headed to the lobby.

I still couldn't believe that I had actually walked through a closed door.

CHAPTER 22

"Dark is the soul that denies the light."

Christmas morning the phone rang waking me. I rolled over to answer it. Who would be calling me at 2:00 AM? It's probably just a wrong number. "Hello," I said in a harsh tone.

"This is Jonathan Stone, the night manager at Riverside Retirement Community. Your Mother has just been taken to St Joseph's Hospital. She's had a heart attack."

I sat up in bed. "When did it happen?"

"Apparently she pulled the emergency cord by the bed which is wired directly to the paramedics. I was away from the front desk at the time, and didn't realize anything happened until they arrived. I don't know her condition."

"I'll call the hospital. Thanks for calling." I said hanging up.

It seemed like an eternity until the operator answered the phone. "Saint Joseph's Hospital, May I help you."

"Could I be connected to the Emergency Room, please?" "One moment, please."

"Emergency Room, Rachel speaking."

"Rachel, this is Jim Roberts. Is Kathryn Roberts in the emergency room," I inquired, my hands shaking.

"Yes, she just arrived. She's in a coma but they are working on her now. I don't know her condition.

"Can I see her?"

"When her condition improves and she's out of emergency you will be able to see her. Let me have your phone number and I will call you when she can see visitors?"

"Okay," I said and gave her my number asking her to call me as soon as possible. I began to pray. The night seemed to last forever. About 5:00 I called again. Another woman answered the phone and couldn't give me any information. She said it was up to the family doctor to talk with me. "He comes in about 8 o'clock," she said.

I didn't want to lose Mom. Who would I confide in? All kinds of thoughts were going through my mind. I felt confused, and my head began to ache. Maybe if I made some coffee I would feel better? I wasn't going to get any more sleep.

I got dressed and went into the kitchen. I had the feeling that Mother was with me but the feeling wasn't good. About 7 the awful feeling went away and I felt peaceful. Surely she was out of danger. I began to relax and tried to read the morning paper. At 8:15 I called the hospital again. This time I got through to Doctor Phillips.

"I was just getting ready to call you," he said. "I have some bad news for you. Your mother passed away about 7 o'clock this morning. She had been in a coma since being brought into E. R. I'm very sorry."

"Thank you," I said as I hung up the phone. Tearing up I thought. 'If I had gone to see her last night when they called I would have been with her. Maybe she'd still be alive, but now it's too late.' It was my fault she was gone. I knew I wasn't responsible, but it felt I was.

I sat in the living room with a box of tissue on my lap, and I cried for some time. I had the wrong interpretation. I thought at seven she was feeling better. I didn't realize that she had given up her body at that time. I've lost her. She's gone forever. At least she was at peace and with Dad now.

I went to the bathroom undressed, turned on the shower, and stepped in the tub as the tears continued. Closing the curtain I let loose with a yell that could have awoken the neighborhood. How could the universe be so cruel? God, you took my Father, my wife, and now my Mother? She was my best friend. At least He didn't get my son. I was angry. No, I was pissed off. What did I do to deserve this punishment? My dark side was winning. I always thought the dark side was the absence of God, how could it also be part of Him? My tears were being washed down the drain as the water run over my face. I hadn't felt this miserable since Doris died. It was like someone had reached in my chest and yanked out my heart. How many times in life does one have to go through such torment?

I began to simmer down feeling a little relieved by the warm water. I turned off the shower, dried off, and got dressed. My day would be busy making the necessary arrangements. I called Shirley and my sons. Eric took it hard. He adored his Grandmother. I felt sorry for him.

After the initial shock and tears, Eric agreed to help me make the necessary arrangements with the minister, the funeral home, the newspaper obituary, and the calling of friends. There was so much to do. He came over for support and to help. I picked up Shirley who took Thursday evening off and we went to the funeral home. We spent an hour welcoming and talking with friends, then, we took our seats in the front pews as the service began.

The minister had wanted me to talk about Mom but I was never able to open my heart in front of people. Eric volunteered to take my place saying he would be honored to talk about his Grandmother. The front pew was reserved for the immediate family. Eric sat to my right on the isle with Shirley. Ellen and Edward sat on my left. They had left their daughter, Stacy, with the baby sitter. Behind us were Charles, Betty and young Jeffrey fidgeting between them. Their older children had chosen not to come. We quietly sat waiting for Reverend Bentley to come to the podium, except for Jeffrey. He was squirming and mumbling softly to himself, yet heard by all.

He yanked on Charles' sleeve, "Daddy, I see angels all around!"

Quietly, Charles responds. "Yes, they like to come to funerals to be with people who are sad."

A minute later, Jeff said. "Who's the dead lady?"

"That's Mr. Robert's Mother. You have to be quiet now," he whispered.

A moment of silence, "Daddy, she wants to tell him something." Jeffrey leaned forward tapping me on the shoulder. I turned around. "Your Mommy wants you to know she's with her soldier man."

Tears began to flow. I think the whole room heard him. It was so quiet that one could hear wings flutter. Charles leaned over pulling Jeffrey back towards him. "You have to be quiet people are trying to pray."

"Okay Daddy, I will."

There was a moment of silence and then Jeffrey started mumbling again. We couldn't quite make out what he was saying, but we were all straining to hear what new gem he was going to present to us. Finally he said. "Do you play ball?"

Jeffrey's dad whispered to him. "You are supposed to be quiet." "There's an angel my size, I wanted to—."

Charles cut him off in mid sentence, and whispered in his ear. "You don't have to talk out loud to angels. Whatever you think they will understand. Now, be quiet."

"Oh," he sat back against the bench and relaxed.

I guessed he was trying to converse with his new spirit friends; if life could just be so simple. I was relieved to be reminded that Mom was with Dad. The fact that Jeffrey mentioned the soldier man validated his ability to see angels and strengthened my belief in the hereafter. Out of the mouths of babes God gives us our lesson for today. I'm sure Mom was pleased.

Reverend Bentley spoke first. We had all contributed to his eulogy except Eric. He had written his own. When his turn came he took the podium and with the emotional strength I never had, gave a fine eulogy.

The Reverend then made an announcement about services for Kathryn O' Reilly-Roberts being held at the church on Saturday at 10:00 AM, and a luncheon being provided afterwards in the social hall of the retirement community where Mrs. Roberts had lived.

One by one we filed by the casket for the last viewing before the lid was closed. It was hard for me letting go. Shirley came up to me and took my hand which sent a wave of moisture streaming down my face. Thank heavens it was almost over.

In the back of the room people were conversing. Doctor Phillips came up to me. "I don't normally go to the funerals of my patients, but your Mother was a patient for twenty years and she was also a friend. I'll miss her. If she had come to see me maybe I could have saved her. Her arteries were badly clogged. I'm sorry for your loss."

"Do you mean Mom didn't keep her appointment," I asked? "No, she hasn't been to see me since her operation."

"She said she had an appointment to see you after the holidays. I know she was having trouble getting her breath and was tiring easily, but I thought she was getting treatment."

"I wish she had. I'm sorry."

"It's not your fault. Mom had a mind of her own. She must have been ready to go. Thank you for coming Doctor, and for taking care of her all these years."

I was glad that the members of my meditation group had also attended. Carolyn gave me some incite about the spirits that were present commenting on little Jeffrey's remarks which she had heard in the back of the room. She explained that the funeral ritual is important because it provides closure for those still living and welcomes the departed back into the spirit world. "It clears the energy so to speak," she said as everyone extended their sympathy and support.

The retirement home where Mom lived had brought a bus full of seniors from the complex. Mom's nearest and dearest friends insisted the community provide transportation. Many of them didn't drive any more, and the others couldn't drive at night.

I was thankful it was over. I thought losing Doris was bad, but losing one's Mother is just as hard on a man as losing his wife. The funeral home would be cremating her tomorrow. She wanted her ashes placed next to her husband in the hills of West Virginia. I would plan a trip back east in the spring.

Edward and Ellen came up to me after the service. "Are you alright Dad?" He inquired giving me a hug, the first hug I had received from him since he was a kid. Maybe the war between us was coming to an end.

"Yes, I made it through okay. I'm glad that you and Eric are emotionally stronger than I am. I guess growing up without a father didn't toughen me up. Your Grandma wasn't a good role model for me on handling emotions."

"Don't be too hard on yourself, Dad. We'll see you Saturday." Ellen gave her condolences and a hug and they were gone.

Marilyn had been in the back of the room and made her way to the front where we were standing. "I'm happy that I had an opportunity to get to know your Mother even for such a short time. But, I didn't get to talk to her about you. She might have had some great stories to tell about you for your book. Thank you for including me." She gave me a hug and left the room.

Eric was the next to say good bye. "I'm very proud of you, son. You gave a great eulogy and you didn't even quiver."

"That comes from standing in front of class day after day talking to thirty college kids."

"You've been acting upbeat lately. Teaching must be good for you, Eric."

"I do enjoy teaching." He paused for a moment then leaned closer and whispered. "Also for the first time I finally realized what it feels like to have feelings for someone."

"I know you loved your Grandmother," I remarked.

"No, Dad, someone else," he said cocking his head as though referring to someone outside.

"You mean—?"

"Yes," he said smiling. "I've got to run so I'll see you on Saturday."

I mused, Eric and Marilyn? Why not? For a moment I forgot about the sorrow I felt. The load had been lifted off my shoulders.

The place had cleared out. I noticed Shirley standing to the side as I glanced around the room. "I guess it's just the two of us left. Thanks for staying. I appreciate having you around giving me moral support. It's been a rough evening." We walked out to the parking lot.

"I'm glad I could be here for you. I'll see you at the funeral service on Saturday. Good night."

"Thanks again, Shirley. Good night." We kissed and hugged, then left.

Friday the day went slowly. I couldn't get my mind off Mom's passing.

* * *

On Saturday we gathered at the church to say our final good-bye to Mom. After the service we all went to the retirement home for lunch. The women had prepared their favorite dishes and put on an appetizing array of food. The mood went from somber to festive, and by the time the meal was over everyone was feeling good.

Eric stood in the corner of the room with Marilyn in deep conversation. He looked at me and winked. It was good to see joyous light at the end of the tunnel after what we had been through this week.

I visited Mom's condo to decide what mementos I wanted to keep and what I wanted to offer to the boys. On Mom's night stand was the picture of Dad in uniform. She hadn't hung the large one I had given her at Christmas. It was still propped up against the wall in the living room. How appropriate I thought, remembering what Jeffrey had said about her being in heaven with her soldier man.

In a dresser drawer was her jewelry box. I hadn't thought of it until I saw it in the box that she wasn't wearing her wedding ring. Was she trying to tell me something? Was it meant for someone else?

* * *

That night I had a date with Shirley. We had planned to go out for Mexican food. One thing about Mexican food, it's served quickly and you are out in an hour. Since it was still early we decided to stop in a night club for a drink. It wasn't really for a drink, it was for the atmosphere. We both drank club soda. There was a band playing so we danced a few before settling back to talk about the funeral.

"Have you given any thought to taking your Mother's ashes back east," she asked?

"I had planned to help out at my old accounting firm during tax season, but after April 15th I'll be free to make the trip. I haven't been on a cross country vacation in years. It might be nice to have someone to travel with me. I don't really want to make the trip alone."

"I know how you feel. I don't like traveling alone either," she commented.

Changing the subject I mentioned, "Shirley, when I was going through Mom's things I found something I want to share with you." Reaching into my pocket I pulled out the rings and handed them to her. Mom wasn't wearing her wedding rings when she died. I found them in the drawer. I thought you might like to wear them."

"Why, Mr. Roberts are you asking me to marry you?" She exclaimed, slipping the rings on her finger.

"Kinda," I paused, then said. "Yes."

"I don't know what to say. I've been single all my life. I care a lot for you, Jim, and I do love you, but I have to think it over. I'm set in my ways you know and just haven't thought of sharing a house with someone. I have all my things just like I want them, and this is so sudden." She went on and on for several minutes. I could tell she was giving my offer serious thought.

Finally I asked, "Is that a yes or no?"

"I don't know." She remarked, all flustered. "It's a maybe. Do you have to know tonight? Can I have more time?"

"Sure, take all the time you want," I said.

We sat at the table listening to the music. I thought, 'Maybe if we sat long enough she'd say, yes,' but she changed the subject.

"I would be happy to go to West Virginia with you though, if you ask me." She said smiling.

My eyes lit up. I hadn't thought of that. Enthusiastically I said. "Oh, yes, I'd be happy to have you go with me. Let's make plans. We'll have so much fun.

When we left the nightclub I noticed the rings were still on her finger. 'Maybe there still is a chance,' I thought. We headed to her place.

CHAPTER 23

*"As unkind as fate can seem in one moment,
it can reward you in the next."*

Eric stopped by the house on Sunday morning. He had something he wanted to discuss with me. Over coffee he proceeded with his important question. "Dad, when did you know you wanted to marry Mom," he asked?

"I knew I wanted your Mom to marry me after our first date, but it was a couple months until I worked up the courage to ask her. I had several conversations with your Grandma before I got the nerve," I said. "Why do you ask?"

"Do you think it's too soon for me to ask Marilyn to marry me?" "Are you ready to spend the rest of your life with the same woman?

"Oh, yes," he replied. "I've never been in love before. I don't know how it should feel, but I have these butterflies in my stomach all the time. I can't stop thinking about her. When I take her home at night I want to stay."

"That's how it feels son. You feel you wouldn't live if you couldn't be with her. I know the feeling well, and I wish you the best. Marilyn is a wonderful woman. I like her a lot and would be proud to have her in the family."

The next day he called again very excited. "Hello, Dad, I popped the question and she said 'Yes'! We're going to get married in June."

"That's great Eric, you need to start planning. If there's anything I can do let me know." I was so happy for him remembering how I felt when I got engaged. It would be a wonderful event. "I'm just sorry your Grandmother never lived long enough to see you married, but I'm sure she'll be there in spirit," I said.

* * *

On Saturday I met Marilyn at the Coffee Shop for the last time. She said, "I think I have enough information to complete your biography. Are there any last words you want to add to your story?"

I thought a moment then said. "There never seems to be an end to a story but what another chapter begins. I lost Doris and thought life was all over. I made my way back; then I met Carolyn and her meditation group. From Eric's accident I met Shirley, and I met you. Offering to write my biography, you convinced me that my life was worthwhile.

Then Mom died and it set me back again. The night of her death my father came to me in spirit and said, 'I've been with you all your life and won't leave until you go with me.' That was comforting.

I plan to take Mom's ashes back to West Virginia soon to put them in my father's vault. Shirley is going with me.

Now I have your wedding to look forward to, and Marilyn, you are certainly welcome in my family."

She smiled. "This is a great new year and so much is happening. I love Eric and look forward to marrying him and being your daughter-in-law. We'll be publishing your biography, Jim," she said. "I promise."

I knew this was going to be a good year. "John's writings are still a mystery to me. Although I helped Charles bury them to keep them out of the wrong hands, I still wanted to read more of them, hopefully this year. Boy, one door never closes but what another opens. I'm grateful for my life. Thank you God." I said.

She clicked off the tape recorder and sighed. "It's finished. Let's celebrate."

Although it was early January, we toasted with our coffee cups to a '***Happy and successful New Year***'.

EPILOGUE

Jim and Shirley made their trip back to the hills of West Virginia. They never officially married and they maintained separate households, but she continued to wear the wedding rings. The evening after Jim's Mom's ashes were placed in the crypt with his dad, they privately recited their vows over a glass of wine at a local restaurant.

Carolyn's Thursday night meditation group continued to meet. Jim and Charles became good friends over the years. As time passed, much of John's writings were revealed to Jim. Charles taught classes at the university on time travel, astral travel, the spirit world, evolution of consciousness, and leading edge thought.

* * *

Eric and Marilyn got married in June, 1992, and their only child, Sarina Roberts, was born a year later. Growing up they encouraged her to keep contact with her spirit family which enabled her to develop psychic abilities. Eric made a career out of astronomy, teaching at the university, and spending time behind the lens of a telescope at the observatory.

* * *

Three years before Eric and Marilyn got married the Martins had given birth to their son, Jeffrey. Charles and Betty soon realized that he was a gifted child, and it would take nurturing and patience to help him develop the unusual talents he displayed. They believed all children had talents to be nurtured, and they wanted their son to have every opportunity to excel. Uncle John's writings lay buried in the field behind their house. Would his talented son one day be able to interpret them?

*   *   *

For thousands of years people have been at war, exhausting the life force of planet Earth. With the evolution of consciousness there was now a *Planet of Hope*. As mankind sees each human being as something to be valued and not killed off, Star Children could bring a thousand years of peace. Will this new millennium bring about a *Planet of Peace?*